We Shall Be Monsters

Christoffer Petersen

We Shall Be Monsters

ISBN: 978-87-93680-16-6

www.christoffer-petersen.com

It is true, we shall be monsters, cut off from all the world; but on that account we shall be more attached to one another.

— Mary Wollstonecraft Shelley (1816-1822)

from Frankenstein; or, The Modern Prometheus

Note to the Reader

We Shall Be Monsters continues the story of retired Police Constable David Maratse. This is the third book in the Greenland Crime series following *Seven Graves, One Winter* (book 1) and *Blood Floe* (book 2). While the story in *We Shall Be Monsters* is resolved, some of the themes explored will continue in book four. While each book deals with a separate story, the characters continue to develop and I intend to explore each character arc over the course of several books. The series is connected, and the reader will enjoy *We Shall Be Monsters* far more if they have read books one and two.

As usual, I blame Maratse.

The people of Greenland speak Greenlandic – including at least four dialects, Danish, and English. In many aspects of daily life, West Greenlandic and Danish are the working languages. *We Shall Be Monsters* is written in British English with the use of some Greenlandic and Danish words used where appropriate, including:

East Greenlandic / West Greenlandic / English
iiji / aap / yes
eeqqi / naamik / no
qujanaq / qujanaq / thank you
Imaqa / maybe

We Shall Be Monsters

Christoffer Petersen

Ataasinngorneq

MONDAY

Chapter 1

There are ridges and knots on the sea ice, like nodes plugged into the dark sea below the hard surface. These crystal webs of primitive communication, blisters of information, create patterns to be read, deciphered; a provocation of fractured threads of ice snaking through Uummannaq fjord, bordered by mountains, cut off by storms, remote, inhospitable for some, a refuge for others.

The taxi's wheels bumped over the ice before settling into another line of communication, the ice road snaking from the village of Uummannaq to the settlement of Saattut to the north and east. The tyres rumbled with the bumps, vibrating through the tired chassis and into the seats. The driver and the Chief of Police sitting next to him smoked cigarettes; thin trails of grey tugged from the smouldering tips, sifted through the harsh black gap at the top of the window. Retired Police Constable David Maratse sat in the back seat, eyes closed, and all but invisible but for the tapping of his fingers on his thigh to the rhythm of the bumps on the ice. The moon lit the fjord all the way to the sharp granite edges and peaks of the mountains, where pockets of darkness waited to spill onto the ice in the wake of a cloud and the moon's passing. The taxi's lights paled in comparison. When the Chief pointed, the driver bumped the taxi out of the grooves and drifted towards the corner of Salliaruseq – the big island. Here, the current ate into the ice and the driver slowed, parking beside the dark blue police Toyota. Constable Aqqa Danielsen waved as he stepped out of the Toyota and onto the ice.

Simonsen, Uummannaq's Chief of Police,

glanced over his shoulder. "We're here," he said.

Maratse opened his eyes, stared past the Chief, through the cracked windscreen, and looked at a shape on the ice, flat and inert, naked and pale beneath the moon. The skin on the back of the body glittered.

"That's not Petra," he said.

"No it's not."

"You said you had found her."

"I did. But this is the first stop."

Simonsen got out of the car and flicked the butt of his cigarette onto the ice. Maratse followed him, fingers still by his side. The thin wind that shivered through Simonsen had no effect on Maratse. He acknowledged Constable Danielsen with a tiny nod as he walked to the body on the ice.

"I found him," the taxi driver said, as he stood beside Maratse.

"Who is it?"

"Salik Erngsen," Simonsen said. "Seventeen years old. He's Anton's boy."

"Anton?" Maratse asked, as he crouched beside Salik's body.

"He manages the fish factory."

"I want to see Petra." Maratse stood up.

"Please," Simonsen said. "Just give me a minute. Tell me what you see."

Maratse scratched his rough fingers on the stiff cloth of his police jacket. He tapped his fingers twice before stuffing his hands into his pockets and looking at Salik. The boy's eyes were frozen open, pocked with spots of frost. There was blood frozen in his nostrils, at the corner of his mouth, and in a deep gash running the length of his left forearm. Maratse leaned over the body and found another cut on the right, dark red, frozen. He frowned as the taxi driver walked past the beam of the headlights, and then he examined the glittering skin on the boy's back. He walked around the body as Simonsen nodded for Danielsen and the taxi driver to step to one side, out of the light. The glitter between streaks of frozen blood on Salik's back was not ice but hooks; barbed fishing hooks used on long lines, baited and snaked on the sea bed to catch halibut. Maratse counted more than thirty, before he leaned closer and pressed the tip of his finger to the end of one of the hooks. He traced a thin length of cotton, frozen taut from the end of the hook to the blood on Salik's back. Each hook had a different coloured thread, blue here, green there, pink, red, orange and purple.

"The colours of the rainbow," Simonsen said. "Do you see the wrists? The blue marks?"

"He was tied?"

"It looks like it."

Maratse looked at Salik's ankles and found more blue marks, a chafing of the skin. He stood up and looked at Simonsen as he lit a cigarette.

"I've looked," Maratse said. "Now, take me to Petra."

"But what do you think?"

"I'm retired."

"I'm asking for your opinion," Simonsen said. "Christ, it's an olive branch for God's sake."

"You're stalling." Maratse walked to the police car. He pointed at Danielsen. "Where is she?"

"Maratse," Simonsen shouted. "I've got a dead boy on the ice with a back full of hooks. I want your opinion."

"Why?"

"Because," he said, his voice softer. "Because you were tortured once."

"This isn't torture," Maratse said. "It's punishment." He flicked his finger at Danielsen. "Take me to Petra."

Danielsen looked at Simonsen, waited for the Chief's nod, and then walked to the police car. Maratse got into the passenger seat and looked straight ahead, past the glittering back of Salik's body, caught in the Toyota's headlights as Danielsen drove around it. The police Constable bumped the Toyota into the parallel grooves of the road to Saattut and drove around the corner of the island. The eastern side of the island was in shadow, the ice black, and the current stronger. Danielsen stopped after half a kilometre.

"We have to walk from here," he said and opened the driver's door.

The air was denser, colder, the bite sharper. Maratse's legs were stiff as he stepped onto the ice, his body heavy and reluctant. He saw a dark hole in the ice and Danielsen led him to it. The hole was rectangular with lengths of wood frozen into the sides. A wooden stand with a drum of fishing line was frozen into the ice on one side of the hole. The line was taut, and Maratse knew there would be a sheet of metal with rocks tied beneath it, down at the bottom of the fjord. He thought of the metal drifting with the current, pulling the line straight as it sank, spreading the halibut hooks. He shook his head free of the image, free of the hooks, and looked to where Danielsen was pointing.

"These are her clothes," he said.

Maratse walked around the fishing hole and peeled the stiff layers of Sergeant Petra Jensen's clothes from the ice. He recognised Petra's blushed mango ski salopettes, ran his fingers across the dark stains of blood spotting the insulated bib. Danielsen tugged at the collar of one of Petra's boots, kicking the heel free of the ice before collecting the pair of boots in his arms. There was a full set of Petra's clothes, including her underwear. Maratse closed his eyes, felt the tug of ice beading around his eyelashes, catching and sticking as he blinked a tear onto his cheek. He remembered the smell of Petra's hair, the warmth of her creamy brown skin, her thin fingers, and her smile. Danielsen carried her clothes to the police car and placed them in a plastic fishing crate in the boot.

"We took pictures," he said, as Maratse handed him the salopettes. "Of everything. Simonsen said I should collect her clothes as soon as you had seen it – the fishing hole."

Maratse picked at the wispy hairs of his light beard; he wouldn't cry, to cry was to accept, to give up. He walked back to the hole in the ice, crouched on one side, and looked more closely at the wooden drum. There were two handles. He stood up and grasped one in each hand. The drum creaked and thumped with uneven spins as he wound the fishing line in, dragging it from the surface of Uummannaq fjord.

"We've done that," Danielsen said. "There was nothing, so we let the fisherman put the line in again."

Maratse ignored him. The drum thumped and the metal squealed in the brackets as he turned the wheel.

The crate laying on one side of the hole was covered in fish blood. Danielsen kicked the crate free of the ice and dragged it to over to Maratse. He tugged a pair of thick gloves from his pocket, and opened the multi-tool on his belt. When Maratse reeled in the first fish Danielsen grabbed it, freed the hook from the lip of the fish with the pliers at the end of the tool and dumped the halibut into the crate. With each fish he brought up Maratse got slower until the crate was full. Danielsen had stacked more fish to one side of the crate. The halibut flopped on the ice, suffocating as the oxygen froze inside their lungs. The metal plate thudded against the wooden spar frozen into the side of the hole. Maratse grabbed it with his bare hands, gripped the line with rocks beneath it, and dragged it onto the ice. He shook the seawater from his hands and stuffed them into his jacket pockets. Danielsen closed the multi-tool and slipped it into the pouch on his belt.

"There's something else," he said, and pulled a sheet of paper from his pocket.

Maratse recognised the handwriting, but the words seemed foreign, without meaning.

"You found this here?"

"That's a copy," Danielsen said. "We found the original in a plastic bag nailed to the side of the fishing wheel. It's her handwriting, isn't it?"

"*Iiji.*"

"And you know what it is?"

Maratse shook his head.

"It's a suicide note."

Maratse folded the paper and slipped it inside his jacket.

"That's evidence."

"It's a copy," Maratse said. He turned towards the corner of Salliaruseq; the taxi lights were just visible in the distance.

"We're calling it a suicide," Danielsen said. "There's nothing to suggest that the two are related; the death of the boy and this…"

"Simonsen thinks so."

"What makes you say that?"

"Why did he show me the boy before you brought me here?"

"I don't know."

"You called me, Aqqa. You told me she'd been taken."

"That's what we thought."

"Then it's not suicide."

"But the note," Danielsen said and pointed at Maratse's pocket. "It's the Sergeant's handwriting."

"Hm."

"I have to call the fisherman," Danielsen said. "This is the second time he needs to collect his catch."

Maratse ignored Danielsen and walked back to the fishing hole. He imagined the fisherman digging the hole with the thick metal blade of his *tuk*, chipping the ice and scattering it across the surface. There was half a plastic bleach bottle screwed into a length of wood hanging from the crossbar beneath the fishing reel. Maratse used it to scoop ice from the hole, peering into the dark sea below. He was no stranger to suicide, but it was rare to find a note, and he could not recall anyone killing themselves by crawling into the sea. Pills and bullets, yes. Hanging and jumping, but never crawling through a fishing hole. Drowning was usually by accident rather than design. Most Greenlanders couldn't or didn't swim, at least the ones he knew. He'd never asked Petra, but whether she could or she couldn't, no-one swam in the sea in winter.

"This is something else," he said, his breath misting into his wispy beard.

He looked over his shoulder and thought about Salik. Maratse tossed the bleach scoop onto the ice, looking up as Danielsen slipped across the ice towards him.

"Simonsen wants us to go back," he said. "If you're ready?"

"*Iiji.*"

"I'm sorry, Maratse. I liked Petra. We all did."

Maratse nodded and walked beside Danielsen to the car.

"She has no family," Danielsen said. "You were the closest one to her. What do you want to do?"

"You say she's dead?"

"*Aap.*"

"Then we bury her," Maratse said. "We'll bury her clothes. In Inussuk."

Pingasunngorneq

WEDNESDAY

Chapter 2

The soft bulb shone through the paper Christmas star in the window, blushing Nivi Winther's cheeks with a red glow. She slipped her mobile into the top drawer of her desk as yet another message of condolence beeped onto the screen. A third message escaped the drawer as Nivi closed it, just as Bibi, her assistant, entered the First Minister's office.

"It's alright, Bibi. I'll look at them later." Nivi gestured at the table. "Just put the coffee there."

"He's waiting in the conference room," Bibi said.

"Then ask him to come in."

Nivi poured two cups of coffee, adding cream to hers as Malik Uutaaq knocked on her door and entered her office.

"Hello Nivi," he said, as he placed his coat over the back of the chair.

"You don't want to hang it up?" She pointed at the coat rack behind the door.

He shrugged, fingering the back of the chair as he waited.

"I don't want this to be awkward, Malik. Please. Sit down." She caught his eye at the sound of a muffled beep seeping out of her desk. "I've been getting them all morning. Friends, family and colleagues who don't think I should have come to work today."

"It is very soon," Malik said. "After what happened."

"Daniel is dead. Tinka is dead too," Nivi said with a slight shake of her head. "I can't bring her back."

"I'm sorry."

"It's okay," she said and sat down. "You knew her; she wouldn't want me to be sad all my life."

"I hardly knew her," Malik said.

"Oh, I wouldn't say that. In some ways you knew her better than I did." Nivi caught her breath for a moment. "I'm sorry. That was uncalled for."

"It's okay."

"It's just hard, you know. Of the two of us, you were the last one to see her."

Malik placed his hands flat on the table. He was quiet as he looked at Nivi, watching her, waiting.

"If it makes you uncomfortable..."

"No," she said. "Stay. There's something I want to discuss."

Malik let out a soft sigh as Nivi straightened her back and tapped her finger on two folders laid out on the table. She waited as he added sugar to his coffee, folding her arms as he took his first sip.

"Like I said at Tinka's funeral, I'm excited about us working together. I would rather work with you than against you. So," she said, and opened the folder, "I have a suggestion, a position I would like you to consider."

"I'm the leader of *Seqinnersoq*. I don't work for you."

"I know that."

"I can't be a part of your government and at the same time lead the opposition."

"A coalition of sorts, we need to be bipartisan, and show strength and unity to bring our people together. To do that we need to be active, to show that what I said in Inussuk was not just empty words. You understand?"

"*Aap.*"

"Good. Then I want you to consider a ministerial post, in my government, not in my party."

"That's unusual."

"It will make people stop and think, that's for sure. And I can't think of a better way to start Christmas than by demonstrating just how serious we are about bridging the gap and serving the people."

"What's the position?"

"Cultural Minister," Nivi said.

"Not fishing and hunting?"

"Do you fish and hunt?"

"A little, sometimes."

"But the people know you for your position on language and identity. Not fishing. Besides, fishing and hunting is taken care of, for the moment at least."

"For the moment. It's a bit of a swing door, or so it seems."

"It's true, it is a demanding post." She sighed. "This is different. I believe with your support, we can appeal to the diversity of the Greenlandic people and," she paused and caught Malik's eye, "tone down the language issue."

"We did agree to that," he said.

"Thank you." Nivi smiled as she slid the folder across the table. "This sets out the way I see the post working. It's a draft for now, we're tweaking some of the language, updating it, but I wanted you to see it first. Why don't you read it through, and I'll see if Bibi can find us some lunch."

Nivi walked out of her office, slowing as soon as she was in the corridor, and out of Malik's sight. Bibi found her there, leaning against the wall, eyes closed, hands shaking.

"Nivi?" she whispered.

"I'm alright, Bibi." Nivi took three slow breaths and opened her eyes. "It's difficult. You understand?"

"Do you want to go home? I can call a taxi."

"No. I have to stay. Please find us some lunch."

Nivi waited until Bibi was gone before returning to her office. Malik had finished his coffee. He poured another as she sat down.

"What do you think?" she asked.

"I'm not the right man for this."

She knew it, of course. For all his rhetoric, his passion for claiming Greenland for Greenlanders, placing so much emphasis on the Greenlandic language, it was all a sham. The reason he never engaged in any other topic, such as housing or employment, topics that really mattered, was that Malik Uutaaq was a poster boy, and nothing more.

But I need him, she thought.

"Are there no other positions?"

"Forgive me, Malik. I'm not sure I understand."

"Let's be honest for a moment, Nivi. You have never rated me highly as a politician, even less as a man." He held his hand up as Nivi started to speak. "It's true that Aarni Aviki was the brains behind *Seqinnersoq*. He ran a good campaign."

"He was a thorn in my side."

"*Aap*," Malik said and smiled. "That's what I paid him for. He would have been perfect for this post."

"You are perfect for this post."

"But I'm not comfortable with it."

"What part?" Nivi asked.

"I think you know."

"Tell me anyway."

Malik leaned over the folder, pushed the top papers aside, and pressed his finger beside the first paragraph on the third page.

"Embracing diversity," he read. "You want me to speak publicly about homosexuality in Greenland?"

"Among other things, yes."

"I can't do that."

"The Danish Prime Minister has embraced the gay culture. He has spoken out about hate crimes. Their Minister of Justice is gay."

"Then give him the post. I won't do it."

"You won't work for me?"

"I won't speak out for gay rights. I can't."

"Why not?"

"I'm a *man*, Nivi."

Nivi scoffed. "I'm aware of that."

"I mean I am a *real* man. I like women."

"A little too much, perhaps," Nivi said. She clenched her fists. "I'm sorry. Say what you want to say."

"If I publicly support diversity in all its forms, I will be laughed at. What will my friends say? My political career will be over."

"Your political career was over the minute Aarni Aviki died. I'm giving you a second chance."

"Only because you need me." Malik brushed the papers to one side. "This tastes like revenge. You're punishing me for sleeping with your daughter."

Malik turned at a knock at the door. Bibi entered the office and the break in their discussion gave Nivi the pause she needed to bury the words she had intended to say, and choose a more diplomatic path. She waited for Bibi to place the sandwiches on the table, nodding her thanks as she left.

"I thought," Nivi said, "that because of Aarni Aviki..."

"You thought because he was gay, that I supported gay rights?"

"Yes."

"Aarni's private life was no concern of mine. We worked well together. He did his job."

"Then I really don't understand."

"Because you're not a man. Because you're more Danish than Greenlandic."

"What's that supposed to mean?"

"It means that just because something is culturally acceptable in Denmark, it doesn't mean it is here. Greenland is its own country, its own people; it has its own culture."

"A diverse culture that includes minority groups, Malik, not just hunters and fishermen. It's people like you who encourage the outside world to think we still live in igloos and turf huts."

"Because that's what sells, Nivi," Malik said, as he stood up. "I'm not as stupid as you think." He pointed at the sea and the snow-lined mountains on the other side of Nuuk fjord. "We've got no oil, and we can't mine without help from other countries. But what we do have is tourism. That's something we can sell. So, forgive me if I want the world to think we are a simple people, living in the Stone Age. The point is we can sell that. That's our future. It's what we can control. You know, in Britain they think of Greenland as *exotic*. A faraway place, off the map. I don't want to disappoint them. I want them to come here and satisfy their curiosity, to send them back home with tall tales so we can fill another cruise ship with ignorant tourists, so we can play the ignorant native and make some money, Nivi. It's all we've got."

"That's what you think?"

"It is."

"And you think presenting a diverse culture will spoil that?"

"I do. It will burst the bubble."

Nivi sat down. She gathered the papers into the folder and leaned back in her chair. She knew the meeting would be difficult, but no-one could have prepared her for this. She thought she knew Malik Uutaaq. She thought she understood his agenda, that it was all about power, but now she realised she underestimated him. His passion surprised her. It was something she could use, something the people needed, something Greenland needed.

"Malik, please sit down."

"I'd prefer to stand." He looked at his watch. "I should be going, anyway."

"Then before you go, tell me, why can't we do both? Why can't we embrace our culture, in all its diversity, *and* play the role of the exotic Greenlander and give the tourists what they want?"

"Because it doesn't work like that."

"You think the tourists read our newspapers?"

"Some might."

"And you think what they read will stop them visiting our country? That's a pretty simplistic view, Malik."

"I'm a simple man, with simple views, Nivi. You knew that."

"My daughter liked you."

Malik sat down and topped up his coffee. He fiddled with the sugar, cursed when he spilled it, the grains scattering over the table.

"She was a little drunk, Nivi. I may have taken advantage of that." Malik looked Nivi in the eye. "I *did* take advantage of that."

"I know."

"And you can still look at me?"

"I would be lying if I said it was easy, Malik. But I need you. The people of Greenland respect you, and even though it hurts me to say that, it's true. You can reach them in ways I can't. They think I'm too close to Denmark."

"You are."

"In some respects. But I'm right about this, you are the right man for this post, and I'll help you. If you bring the people together."

"I need some time."

"I want to make an announcement before Christmas."

"That's ten days."

The phone on Nivi's desk rang, and she lifted her finger, gesturing for Malik to wait as she answered it. He watched her, saw her cheeks pale as she pressed the receiver to her ear.

"What is it, Nivi?"

"That was Lars Andersen, the Police Commissioner."

"*Aap?*"

"You remember Sergeant Petra Jensen? They found her clothes beside a hole in the ice a few days ago, with a suicide note. She's dead, and she's going to be buried in Inussuk, right next to Tinka."

Chapter 3

Qitu Kalia stood in front of *Katuaq*, Nuuk's Cultural Centre, and kicked the snow from his shoes. He plucked his hearing aids from the inside pocket of his jacket and pressed one into each ear. The waitress behind the counter of the café smiled as she recognised him and tapped her ear.

"Are they new?"

"*Aap*," he said.

"And we can speak Greenlandic now?"

"I can *hear* Greenlandic now. It makes it easier to lip read."

Qitu frowned as the waitress whispered, gesturing for him to lean over the counter.

"Latte is Italian," she said, smiling as she prepared his usual order.

Qitu felt his cheeks blush. He paid and pointed to a seat by the window, tugging his *MacBook Air* from his satchel as he sat down. He remembered a recent visit to the new Gymnasium building, when he was writing a piece about the academic reform plaguing lecturers and confusing students. The examination hall had glowed with white apples, as the majority of students made the most of VAT-free computers bought in Denmark. Although, there was a fine line between aesthetically pleasing and robust in Greenland and the latter cost less in the long run. Qitu smiled as he felt the tap of the waitress's shoes along the floor.

"*Qujanaq*," he said, as she put his latte beside his computer.

Qitu opened his email and checked the time of his meeting. A quick look at the clock on the screen confirmed he was early, so he opened the rough draft of his latest assignment.

The door opened and a young woman scuffed her way into the café. Qitu lifted his head at the prick of cold air on his skin and watched as the woman drifted past the counter to a seat a few tables away from him. He had seen her before; he recognised the black whalebone studs in her ears, her lips, and her nose. The two large studs in the skin below her bottom lip caught his eye, tusk-like they jutted out above her chin. The rest of her outfit was black, which made her pink hair all the more shocking. She caught Qitu's eye and he quickly dipped his head, allowing the glare of the screen to consume him.

She was still staring when he looked up a second later, and again when another guest entered the café. Qitu knew the man by name and waved him over.

"It's good to see you, Qitu," the man said.

"You too, Palu."

Palu Didriksen glanced at the woman with pink hair and then pulled out a chair.

"I'm glad we could meet. I thought you would be busy in the run up to Christmas."

Qitu studied Palu's lips, and then nodded.

"I have been busy. You heard about Nivi Winther's daughter?"

"I was in Denmark and Germany, but yes, I heard. Shocking."

"It was very sad."

"But it has shaken up the politicians, eh?"

"*Aap.*"

"Weren't you working on a piece about Malik Uutaaq? What happened to that?"

"I stopped. It didn't seem right. Daniel Tukku

commissioned it."

"He was the one who killed the girl?"

"And kidnapped the First Minister."

"I understand." Palu leaned over the table and gestured for Qitu to close his computer. "Did you hear anything about what happened in Berlin?"

"Rumours about Greenlandic police involved in a shoot-out. Nothing was confirmed."

Palu nodded. "It was all covered up. Quite well, actually."

Qitu remembered trying to get a comment from the Police Commissioner in Nuuk, but had been unsuccessful. The deadline for the Nivi Winther piece had forced him to drop the investigation and concentrate on something much closer to home. But he did remember hearing something about Sergeant Petra Jensen and David Maratse – the busiest retired police Constable he knew. The thought made Qitu smile.

"I was invited to Berlin to meet with Aleksander Berndt. He used to be the CEO of the Berndt Media Group, but has since been replaced," Palu continued.

"Why?"

"That was part of the cover-up. Berndt was involved in the shoot-out in Berlin. So, we never met. But, I got a call on the morning I was leaving, and I met with the new CEO's assistant."

"What about?"

"That's what I'm coming to."

Qitu tilted his head to one side to look past his friend. The young woman with the tusks was still watching him. She hadn't ordered anything and the waitress avoided her table.

"You're not listening, Qitu."

"Sorry," Qitu said. He fiddled with his hearing aids, and focused on Palu's lips.

"Berndt wanted to invest in Greenland, but when it was revealed he was more interested in exploiting Greenland than helping it, the new CEO stepped up and made me another offer."

"I thought you met with his assistant?"

"I did, and he said that instead of investing, the Berndt Media Group would make a donation, to support a new company, with no strings attached, no agenda, and only two conditions."

"And they are?"

"That the company is a media company, digital first, print later, and that they investigate stories that affect the people of Greenland, independently of government or business." Palu leaned back in his chair and grinned. He stabbed his chest with his thumb. "You're looking at the new CEO of NMG."

"What?"

"Nuuk Media Group." Palu waved his hands. "I know, not very original, but that's not important. The thing is I have the money and the office space. I even have a story. All I need is an investigative reporter to write for me."

"You want me to work for you?"

"I'll pay you twice what *Sermitsiaq* is paying."

"I don't know."

"You're thinking about your future? This *is* your future. I've got enough funding for three years. I think the CEO was embarrassed by the whole Berndt affair. He wants to make up for it."

"And what's the story?"

Palu jerked his head backwards, flicking his eyes to one side.

"The girl," he whispered when Qitu frowned.

"The one with the..."

"Pink hair and tusks, yes." He held two crooked fingers in front of his chin.

Qitu looked at the girl, caught a glimpse of her fingers as they shrank inside the long sleeves of her hoodie, and then focused on her face. She wore no make-up that he could see and she was familiar. He had seen her before, but struggled to remember where. Then it came to him, when he was researching the Malik Uutaaq story in *Mutten*, she had been working behind the bar on Nuuk's main street. He remembered the pink hair, although the tusks were new.

"What's her name?" he asked.

"Tertu," Palu said. "I'll call her over."

When she stood Qitu was surprised at how tall she was. He looked at her heels and saw the flat soles of her boots; they left wet prints on the tiled floor. The rubber squeaked as she sat down.

"I know you," she said. "You're the journalist. You wrote about Tinka."

"Did you know her?"

"No."

Qitu studied her face; saw the lighter complexion, the colour of skin that resulted in the death of Tinka Winther. Tertu spoke in Danish, and he wondered how much Greenlandic she knew.

"I choose to speak Danish," she said. "It's quicker."

"But your mother?"

"Is Danish. I speak Greenlandic when I don't want her to understand. English when I don't want my dad to understand." She stared at Qitu and whispered; the tusks above her chin moved more than her lips.

"What did you say?"

"I said in your case I'll whisper."

"I told you we could trust him, Tertu," Palu said.

"I don't trust anyone."

"Why?" Qitu asked.

He had other questions that started with *why*. Why the tusks? Why the black clothes? Why the attitude? Why did she hide her hands? And why did her cheeks tic, just below her eyes, when she saw him looking at her cuffs?

Tertu glanced at Palu.

"I can't tell him."

"We agreed, Tertu."

"He could be police."

"He's not."

Qitu caught himself staring. There was something fascinating about her, beneath the surface. The journalist in him was curious; perhaps even enough to quit his steady job and to work for Palu and the Nuuk Media Group. They would need a new name, something to match the story he imagined, hoped even, that the girl was reluctant to tell.

"You want to know if you can trust me?" Qitu asked. "How about this?"

He rolled back his sleeve and held his arm beneath the bulb of the lamp hanging above the table. He circled three round blemishes in the soft crook of his arm.

"I was in Copenhagen when I was younger, sleeping rough for a while. I missed my home. I did this," he said, and tapped his arm, "to forget." Qitu rolled down his sleeve and nodded at Tertu's fingers.

"Most young people cut their inner arms, or thighs, when they want to forget. Is that why you're hiding your hands?"

Tertu teased two fingers out of her sleeve and pulled back the cuff to reveal one hand. The skin between her knuckles was striped with two black bands joined with diagonal lines. Qitu smiled as he recognised the traditional stick and poke tattoos of the Inuit. Tertu rolled back both her cuffs to reveal more bands above the middle knuckle. She had bands wrapped around her wrists too.

"Greenlandic?" he asked.

"Aleut. When I was fifteen I went to the Inuit Games in Alaska. I did some there, more at home."

"I like them."

"Show him," Palu said.

Tertu turned her hands and held her palms upwards, tilting them towards the light. There were more bands between the knuckles on the inside of her fingers. Unlike the bands on the front, these were different colours. Ink from the bands bled into the skin, as if the tattooist was not a professional, a *scratcher* in a hurry. The bands were linked with jabs of ink, large and small, splintered as if the bone needle was fractured. Tertu's skin was blistered with assorted welts of raised skin; her little fingers were curled as if the nerves had been pinned.

"Two more," she said, and pricked her thumbnail against the empty spaces between the joints of the second and third fingers of both hands.

"Two more what?"

"Until I am free."

"I don't understand," Qitu said.

Tertu slipped her hands inside her cuffs and

nodded for Palu to speak.

"Each tattoo is a mark. Just like the loyalty cards they give out in the cafés in Denmark."

"*Aap?*"

"When the card is full, you get a free coffee. Here," Palu said with a nod towards Tertu's hands, "when her hands are full, she is free."

"Free from what?"

Palu gestured for Qitu to come closer.

"You know how society looks at homosexuality in Greenland?"

"We have Gay Pride in Nuuk..."

"And Sisimiut and a few other towns, but in the small villages and settlements, it is taboo. Young people have needs and others are exploiting them. Tertu is *qaleralik.*"

"Halibut?"

"She's treated like a flat fish, a bottom feeder. The lowest of the low. The marks on her fingers are made with paint and fish hooks. When a man or woman wants sex with someone of the same sex, they go fishing. Tertu's bills are paid – just enough to keep her afloat, but not enough to let her swim, not until her debt is paid, and her fingers are full. I paid for her to come to Nuuk. To get her away from the settlement she lives in."

"And she's gay?" Qitu looked at Tertu.

"Yes."

"I still don't understand."

Tertu held up her hand and pointed at the two empty spaces.

"I have two times left."

"And then you are free?"

"Free?" she laughed. "When my fingers are full

he will kill me."

"Who will?"

"The man I want you to investigate," Palu said. "This is big, Qitu. There is a man controlling this underground world of sex. He finds vulnerable people and promises to protect them. He says the marks are bands of loyalty, but Tertu has never met anyone with all their fingers banded."

"He kills them?"

"Maybe," Tertu said. "Or maybe the client kills them."

"Client?"

"The ones paying for sex."

"But you said you would be free, Tertu. Death isn't freedom."

"No," she said, "just preferable. He can't hurt you when you're dead."

"And you escaped."

"I don't want to die."

Tertu held Qitu's gaze for a moment before looking away.

"Qitu," Palu said. "This is the kind of story NMG needs to investigate. The kind that can change lives. Will you take the job?"

Qitu caught Tertu's eye and nodded.

Chapter 4

Gaba Alatak rolled back the duvet and swung his legs over the side of the bed. The woman beside him turned onto her side. He ignored her, walked to the bathroom and took a long shower, rinsing the woman's scent off his body. He let the towel drop to the floor and shaved, clipped an errant hair from his nostril, and rubbed a light oil into his scalp. *Bald is strong,* he thought. So very different from the thick hair that made him look half his age. He would let it grow when he was older, somewhere past middle age. Gaba picked up the towel and hung it over the rack, grabbing his phone from the kitchen counter as he made coffee. It was still dark. He checked his messages in front of the window looking out over old Nuuk as the coffee machine spluttered behind him.

"Miki," he said, when his partner answered his phone. "Training at nine. Get everyone."

"What about Atii?"

"I'll pick her up," Gaba said and glanced at the door to the bedroom.

He took a fresh mug of coffee into the bedroom, climbed onto the bed and wafted it beneath Constable Atii Napa's nose.

"Time to get up," he said.

"Too early."

Gaba put the mug down on the bedside table, crawled off the bed and whipped the duvet off Atii's body.

"What are you doing?" she said, clawing at the duvet, but Gaba pulled it out of her reach.

"Come on. You'll be late."

"For what?"

"SRU training. You've got five minutes."

Gaba dressed, fixed two plates of toast, and waited for Atii to pad out of the bedroom and into the shower. He banged on the door a minute later.

"Two minutes, and we're leaving."

"You're a bastard, Gaba Alatak."

"What's that?" Gaba said, as he opened the door.

"I said, you're a bastard, *Sergeant* Alatak."

"Of course I am. Now get ready. We leave in one minute."

Gaba turned off the coffee machine and grabbed his car keys. He took the stairs, kicked at the stone someone had propped the security door open with, and walked to his car. The Northern Lights drifted across the December sky as Gaba started the car and scraped the ice off the windows.

"At last she decides to show up," he said, as Atii jogged across the parking area, a piece of toast between her teeth as she fiddled with the utility belt around her waist. She flicked him the finger as she opened the door and sat in the passenger seat.

"You could have given me more warning."

"You could have set an alarm."

"But you had time to shower, shave and oil your bloody head."

"*Aap.*"

"You had time to do all that."

"Because I set an alarm," Gaba said, as he put the car in reverse and backed out of the parking space.

The snow crunched beneath the thick winter tyres as Gaba accelerated onto the road and sped down the hill from the tower blocks of Qinngorput and past the school below. It would take five minutes to drive into the town centre, fifteen in total to the training area. Atii finished her toast and wrangled her wet hair into a ponytail as Gaba drove.

"She was right," she said.

"Who?"

"Petra said you were a bastard."

"Constable Napa," Gaba said. "Did you or did you not have a good night?"

"*Aap.*"

"Was I or was I not a good lay?"

"What?"

"Answer the question, Constable." Gaba slowed at the roundabout by the docks and accelerated out of it. "Was I a satisfactory hump?"

"You were."

"And did you, at any time, regret pleading for me to take you home?"

"Pleading?"

"That's how I remember it."

"I did not plead."

"Well that's not what I will be telling the boys."

"You'd better not," Atii said, as she balled her hand into a fist and thumped Gaba's arm.

"We share everything."

"Bastard."

"I tell you what," Gaba said. "Give me ten perfect groupings with an MP5 on the range today and I will keep my mouth shut."

"Ten?"

"That's right."

"Perfect groupings?"

"Three rounds inside centre circle, ten times. That's thirty rounds, Constable."

Atii muttered as Gaba slowed for a bus.

"What's that?"

"I said *fine*. You're on."

"Good."

"And you're buying dinner. Regardless."

"We'll see about that."

Gaba pulled up beside Miki Satorana's police car four minutes later and waved at the younger policeman. He shrugged when Miki nodded at Atii in the passenger seat.

"We have a deal, Sergeant," Atii said, as she got out of the car. She grabbed her jacket from the back seat and walked across the compacted snow to the training hut.

Gaba winked at Miki and walked with him around the hut to the firing range. He inspected the FBI-style targets Miki had set up thirty metres from the firing line. He nodded and gestured towards the hut.

"Peter, the new guy, is coming later," Miki said. "He had the night shift."

"And Tiguaq?"

"He's sick. He showed up but I sent him home."

"Why?"

"Because he's sick," Miki said. "And I don't want to catch it, whatever it is."

Gaba slapped Miki on the back and followed him inside the training hut. There were four MP5s on the table, and a fifth that Atii assembled as Miki made coffee. Gaba watched her work, nodding as she placed the machine pistol on the table and got to work on loading the thirty-round magazines. Miki handed her a mug of coffee when she was finished.

The SRU – the Greenlandic Police Special Response Unit – was small enough to fit inside the *King Air* twin turboprop aircraft that Air Greenland made available for emergencies all over the country. Usually the emergencies were medical, but if the Commissioner determined that the SRU was required, then they would go wherever and do whatever it took. The last non-medical sortie was when Miki and Gaba had flown to Uummannaq in search of the First Minister. The team was small but well-trained, and Atii, the newest member of the SRU, was a welcome addition, a fact that Gaba reminded himself about, on and off duty. When Atii was finished with the first five groupings, and Gaba had inspected them, he decided to change the rules.

"Twenty groupings," he said. "At forty-five metres."

Atii shook her head and laughed. "Why don't I just tell Miki that we had sex last night and be done with it?"

Miki rolled his eyes and waited for Gaba's signal to fire.

"Fifteen and I won't say how good you were," Gaba said.

"How about this, Sergeant," Atii said. "If you can make a perfect grouping at fifty metres, I won't tell Miki about what I did to you with the..."

"Stop," Miki said. "I really, *really* don't want to hear it." He pointed at the range. "But I'll give one hundred kroner to whoever can put three in a group at one hundred metres."

Gaba stared downrange towards the sea. "Is the range long enough?"

"You see the barrel?"

"Yes."

"That's eighty. The range dips after that. But if we put a target on top of the barrel and move it another twenty, we should just about be able to see it."

"Just about?" Atii said.

"Yeah."

"Alright," Gaba said. "Let's do it."

Constable Peter Iikkila waved from the deck of the training hut as the three SRU members walked back along the range to the firing line.

"What are we shooting?" he asked, as Gaba shook his hand.

"Group of three at one hundred metres," he said, and looked up. "In the snow."

"Is that standard?"

"*Naamik*," Miki said. "But it's the only way I could get Atii to shut up about her sexual exploits with the boss."

"Thank you, Miki," Gaba said. "Welcome to the SRU, Peter. Now grab an MP5 and let's see what you can do."

"It's an elimination round," Miki said, as soon as they were all ready. "You miss with one bullet, you're out. Each bullet on target, and in the circle," he said, tapping the spotting scope on the tripod beside him, "gets you through to the next round. Boss? You first?"

"Alright," Gaba said, and walked up to firing line.

"Wait a second," Miki said and held out his hand. "You want to play, you've got to pay."

Gaba fished a one hundred kroner note from his wallet and slapped it into Miki's hand. He winked at Peter, and shouldered the MP5. Flakes of snow flurried across the range, and Gaba waited for a second, aimed, and fired. Miki checked the scope, sucked a breath of air through his teeth, and then moved to one side as Atii pressed her eye to the eyepiece.

"It was the snow," Gaba said, and slapped Peter on the back. "Your turn."

Atii hid a smile behind her hand and turned away as Gaba stared at her.

Peter's shot went wide and Miki pressed the two notes into his pocket.

"I'm just keeping them safe," he said, when Gaba pointed at him.

Atii pressed her money into Miki's hand and took aim. She shrugged when Gaba checked the shot.

"Dead centre," he said.

"That's not what you said last night," Atii said, and giggled.

"Please," Miki said. "I'm shooting."

The four SRU members took it in turns to check Miki and Atii's shots. None of them heard the car pull up outside the hut. Nor did they notice Police Commissioner Lars Andersen as he stepped out of the hut and onto the firing range.

"Sir," Gaba said when he heard the Commissioner's discreet cough.

"Can I have a quick word, Sergeant?"

"Yes, sir."

Gaba pressed his MP5 into Peter's hands and followed the Commissioner inside the hut. He sat down at a nod from the Commissioner.

"What's this about?"

"There's no easy way to say this, Gaba, so I'll make it quick. Petra Jensen is dead. It's suicide. Her clothes were found at a hole in the ice in Uummannaq."

"Petra wouldn't..."

"Together with a note." The Commissioner paused. "It was her handwriting, Sergeant."

"You're sure?"

"Simonsen called earlier. He said that Maratse confirmed the clothes are Petra's and the note was written by her hand. There's not much else to go on. According to Simonsen's Constable."

"Aqqa."

The Commissioner nodded. "According to Aqqa, Petra was last seen outside the store in Uummannaq two days ago. Apparently, she struggled with a man, and was taken against her will."

"Then it's not suicide."

"We don't know that."

"Has Simonsen picked up this man?"

"He can't find him."

"Do we have a name?"

"Just wait, Gaba."

"Sir," Gaba said. He stood up. "Do we have a name?"

"It's poor evidence at best. The eyewitness was drunk."

"All I need is a name."

"And if I give it to you?"

"I'll be on the first flight north, sir."

"Well, that's lucky, because I have three seats on the morning flight to Ilulissat tomorrow morning. We change there and fly on to Qaarsut. Simonsen will drive us to Inussuk. They are burying Petra's clothes. A symbolic gesture, I suppose."

"What does Maratse say?"

"He's the one who arranged the funeral."

"He hasn't asked for any details?"

"No, and Simonsen has promised not to give him

any. We're concerned that he might take matters into his own hands."

"Might?"

"Listen, Gaba, this is Simonsen's case. He's in charge. The last thing he needs is a retired Constable and the leader of the SRU hunting down a man who may or may not be involved in Petra's death." The Commissioner looked up at a cheer from the firing line. "That's Atii, isn't it?"

"Yes, sir."

"It looks like she won. What was the distance?"

"One hundred metres."

"A group of three?"

"*Aap.*"

"Well, you can console Miki by telling him to pack."

"He's coming with us?"

"I'm temporarily assigning him to Simonsen. Once we're finished with the funeral, he will help with the investigation. Petra meant a lot to me, too, Gaba. I trust Simonsen's judgement on keeping you and Maratse out of the loop. But I also trust Miki to report back to you with regular updates. Until then, pack your bags. I'll see you at the airport tomorrow morning."

Sisamanngorneq

THURSDAY

Chapter 5

Nanna followed Maratse around for most of the day, sitting beside him when he sat on the deck of his house and drank coffee, running alongside him as he strode from the house to the dogs, and holding his hand as he walked up the mountainside to the graveyard overlooking the fjord to one side and the settlement of Inussuk to the other. Sisse, Nanna's mother, joined them in the graveyard, stroked Nanna's hair and fixed her hat so it covered her ears. She lifted Nanna onto her lap as she sat down on the bench beside Maratse.

"I hope Nanna hasn't been bothering you," she said.

"No bother," Maratse said and smiled.

"David, I just don't know what to say." Sisse took Maratse's hand. "It's just so terrible. Petra was such a wonderful woman. And what you had..." She let go of his hand. "I'm sorry."

Maratse nodded. "How is Buuti?" he asked.

"She's busy," Sisse said with a nod.

"I told her not to make a fuss."

"Not to make a fuss?" Sisse laughed softly. "The First Minister is coming to the funeral. And the Police Commissioner. What on earth made you think she wouldn't make a fuss?"

"Hm."

Sisse waited for Maratse to speak.

"I gave money to Nikoline in the store and made her promise not to take any money from Buuti or Karl for the food," Maratse said.

"That's clever, but what if Karl drives into town on his snow scooter to get everything?"

Maratse reached into his pocket and pulled out a set of keys. He placed them in Sisse's hand.

"You can tell him you found them in the snow. He'll be pleased."

Sisse smiled and tucked the keys into her pocket.

"I have to go. I promised to help Klara with cakes for the wake."

"*Qujanaq.*"

"It's the least we can do, David. I only wish I could do something for you."

"You are," he said. "And I have enjoyed Nanna's company."

The sound of the De Havilland Dash 7 approaching the gravel strip airport in Qaarsut made them look up. Nanna leaped off her mother's lap and pointed at the lights.

"Do you think the First Minister is on the plane?" Sisse said.

"*Iiji.* Maybe her secretary too. And Malik Uutaaq."

"We'd better be off then. Come, Nanna. Let's go and help Klara in the kitchen."

Nanna waved at Maratse and then led Sisse down the path to the settlement below. Maratse waited until they were gone before walking over to Tinka Winther's grave. He looked into the open grave beside it. No-one had questioned why he wanted to bury Petra's clothes in Inussuk. Nor did they wonder at the timing, only a few days since her clothes were found on the ice, together with the note. Maratse pulled the note from his pocket and turned it in the moonlight to read it. The writing was thin, the letters scrawled and shaky. Exhibiting signs of stress, according to the report Simonsen received from the forensic expert in Nuuk. Danielsen had told him about it when they drove back to Uummannaq, across the ice. He said that Simonsen wanted to be sure before they told him.

Maratse lowered the note in his hand. The forensic report had come through quickly. Too quickly. The expert had missed something in Petra's signature. Maratse didn't blame him, the man didn't know Petra, wouldn't know how she usually signed her name, and he couldn't know that the only person who called her by her Greenlandic name was Maratse.

Piitalaat.

She had written it for him.

It was what gave him hope. And, as soon as the funeral was over, once the grieving process had begun and everyone had accepted Petra was gone, Maratse could begin his search, and bring her back from the dead.

He grunted at the sound of footsteps in the snow and folded the note back into his pocket.

"Sisse said you were up here," Karl said. He tapped two cigarettes out of the packet in his hand and offered one to Maratse.

"I quit," he said with a smile. "Petra made me."

"Petra? You usually call her…"

"Piitalaat." Maratse nodded. "You're right."

Karl lit his cigarette and puffed a small cloud of smoke over the fjord.

"We dug seven graves before the winter," he said. "Edvard's niece." Karl pointed to the tiny plot for the stillborn child. "Tinka Winther. Piitalaat," he said with a nod to the open grave next to Maratse. "Buuti is so sad. Nukannguaq has to wipe Buuti's eyes as she bakes. We are all sad."

"*Iiji.*"

"All of us. But not you, David."

"What do you mean?"

"I mean you look sad, but then you always look sad." Karl grinned behind another cloud of smoke. "But here we are in the graveyard, standing by Petra's grave, and you are not sad. Why?"

Maratse shrugged.

"Okay, tell me something else."

"What?"

"Why is your sledge packed for a long trip? Why are my bearskin trousers in your closet? And why is my rifle oiled? Why does it have a new sling?"

"It needed it."

"When did you take it?"

"I bought oil in Uummannaq when Danielsen dropped me off. Why?"

"I couldn't find it for about a week. I thought Edvard had it." Karl shrugged. "Anything else?"

"You forgot the shooting screen," Maratse said.

"You've taken that too?"

"*Iiji.*"

"And where are you going?"

"I need to get away for a while."

"Where?"

"I don't know."

"You don't think she's dead, do you?"

"Karl," Maratse said and lowered his voice. "You can't say anything. You can't tell anyone."

"But if you think she is alive, you have to tell the police."

Maratse shook his head.

"Simonsen has another investigation to take care of. He won't have time for Petra."

"Not for a suicide, but if you think she is alive."

"No, Karl. I need to do this my way. It will be quicker."

The sound of a taxi on the ice below them turned Maratse's head. He spotted the headlights as they snaked between the icebergs frozen into the fjord. Two more cars followed the taxi. Maratse nodded towards the path and led Karl down the mountainside.

"You'll carry the coffin with me?" he asked.

"You mean, will I play my part?"

"*Iiji*, for Piitalaat."

"I'll do anything for Petra." Karl paused at the top of the path. "I can come with you."

"*Eeqqi*. I need to do this alone."

Maratse said nothing more until they reached the bottom of the path. The black sand beneath the snow cast a grey pallor over the well-trodden path to the houses. Maratse could see Buuti in the window, lighting candles. Nukannguaq bustled at the table behind her, while Sisse, Nanna and Klara carried cakes up the steps to the house. Maratse felt a pang of guilt turn in his stomach as he thought about the deception. He stopped and pressed his hand against Karl's chest.

"You can't tell anyone. Not even Buuti."

"She will understand."

"She wouldn't, Karl. No-one will, and no-one must know. I think I know who might have taken Piitalaat. I can't let anyone stop me."

"You're that sure she's alive?"

Maratse glanced at three pairs of headlights as they parked on the ice. The passengers walked up and over the ice foot and onto the beach.

"*Iiji,*" he said, and walked down the beach to greet Greenland's First Minister, and the rest of the guests for the funeral of Sergeant Petra Jensen.

There was no church service. The priest from Uummannaq laid Petra's coffin into the ground with all the solemnity the occasion demanded; a coffin with no body, just a set of clothes. It was Nivi Winther's words that caused even the most stoic of the congregation to shed a tear. All but Maratse. He was the last to leave the graveyard. Gaba Alatak met him on the path to the houses below.

"I'm sorry for your loss," he said, and shook Maratse's hand.

"And yours. She was your friend too."

"I'd like to think so." Gaba waved for Miki to go on without him. He walked with Maratse down the path and stopped at the beach. "Before we go inside," he said, "there's something you need to know."

Maratse waited. Karl's house was small, and soon filled with the people of Inussuk and the few guests with their entourage. A group of men smoked on the deck outside, close enough to hear what might be said on a cold, windless night. Gaba plucked at Maratse's elbow and nodded for him to walk further along the beach.

"Simonsen isn't telling you anything, is he?"

"Petra committed suicide. He has closed the case."

"That's what he wants you to think. The Commissioner told me there is a witness. Someone in town. I can find out who it is. Then, maybe we can pay them a visit. We can find out what really happened to Petra."

"Are you staying to help with the investigation?"

"No, but Miki is. You know about the boy who was killed, Salik Erngsen. That's Miki's assignment, but he's going to report everything to me."

"But you'll be in Nuuk."

"I will. But I can fly here..." Gaba coughed. "Anytime," he said.

Gaba's eyes glistened in the moonlight, and Maratse looked away to give the SRU leader a moment. He remembered Petra's outburst about Gaba when she picked him up at the hospital in Nuuk. Something about Gaba's infidelity. That was the first time Maratse had seen her angry. She had a fire in her eyes that burned so brightly. His stomach twisted again, and he could almost feel the tick of the watch on his wrist, thudding through his body. He was wasting time. The charade needed to end now, so that everybody, Gaba included, could drift away and grieve in their own time, and give Maratse the space and time he needed to bring her back. He shoved all thoughts of what Petra might be experiencing to one side. He couldn't think of that. He just had to act, and the sooner the better.

"If there's anything I can do. If you need anything."

Maratse realised Gaba was speaking to him, and he shook his head.

"I'm fine."

"Okay," Gaba said, and nodded towards the house. "We had better go inside." He paused at the sight of a fully-laden sledge and the dog team chained beside it. "Someone is going hunting," he said.

"*Iiji.*"

"Someone you know?"

"I don't know them," Maratse said, as he walked beside Gaba to the house.

Nivi Winther met them on the deck and Gaba excused himself, leaving the First Minister and Maratse alone.

"I'm so sorry, David. I know that Petra was very special to you."

"*Qujanaq.*" Maratse stiffened slightly as Nivi hugged him, and then he smiled. "Your words were very nice," he said and pointed up at the mountainside. "I think everybody appreciated them."

"It was the least I could do. It was you and Sergeant Jensen who found Tinka for me. You brought her home. I plan on visiting Tinka often, when work allows. I know Tinka will watch out for Petra. They can keep each other safe."

Maratse ignored the twist in his stomach and nodded.

"You must be cold," Nivi said. "Let's go inside."

The tick of the second hand struck hammer blows inside Maratse's body as he shook hands, hugged, and mumbled thanks to the mourners, his neighbours and friends. Simonsen shook his hand and the Commissioner took him to one side. Maratse had to concentrate to hear his words over the thundering of the watch on his wrist.

It was Karl who saved him, as he apologised to the Commissioner and guided Maratse into the kitchen and out of the back door.

"Your clothes are in the shed," he said. "The rifle too."

"I have to wait until they have gone, at least."

"*Naamik,*" Karl said with a shake of his head. "You need to find Piitalaat. Now go," he said, and pushed Maratse towards the shed. "I'll tell people it was too much, that you needed some time for yourself."

"You'll help me apologise to Buuti?"

"Bring Petra back and you won't have to." Karl curled his finger and thumb to his ear. "You'll call me if you need me?"

"*Iiji.*"

Karl nodded. "Good hunting," he said, and closed the kitchen door.

Chapter 6

Sergeant Petra Jensen's breath misted over her body, cooling and beading on the rusted bracelets cuffing her wrists. The tattered jeans she wore were long enough to cover her ankles if she pointed her toes, but too large to provide any warmth around her waist. Her stomach was bare, like her chest, her neck, and her arms. The fine hairs on her skin prickled in the cool air. She rested her head on her arm, felt the pull on her wrists as the bracelets rattled against the chain hooked above her head on a nail bent into the thin wooden wall. She breathed again, another cloud of warm breath, condensing around her body. She looked through the cloud and saw the red eye of the camera staring at her, unblinking, unmoving, penetrating, vibrating slightly to the insistent thump of the diesel generator juddering on the rocks outside. She twisted at the sound of someone kicking the snow from their boots, unlocking the padlock on the door, dragging the chain, one link at a time, through the iron rings on the door and the frame. The freezing air from the ice rushed in to mix with the cold air in the cabin, followed by the man in the parka, his head funnelled and hidden inside his hood like a trunk, and the tools he carried in front of him were the tusks. A hideous elephant, silent but for the thump of its feet and the rattle of the chain.

He ignored Petra, dumping the tools on the floor beside the legs of the tripod before turning the camera off. She heard the click of the back cover being removed, the thick shush of sleeves rubbing against the man's sides as he swapped the SD card in the camera for another. He closed the cover with a click. The camera beeped as he turned it on and Petra held her breath.

The screen glowed for the few seconds it took the man to setup the camera and focus the lens on Petra. A few seconds in which she could see the fibres of the fur ruff lining his parka, the elephantine extension of his head, and the wet sheen of the man's eyes deep within the tubular shadow of his hood.

This was the third card change in a row since he last touched her, when he forced three spoons of sticky oatmeal into her mouth, splashed her lips with water. He would touch her again, the next time he changed the card. The fourth time. Four was important. No matter how much it hurt when he twisted her skin between his fingers, when he tightened the chain, the fourth time was contact, and she dreaded and longed for it, in the tragic way that contact, *any* contact, connected her with the real world, not the dark, solitary, freezing claustrophobia of captivity.

She moved her head as he retreated from the camera, and the screen's glow diffused in the black of the cabin. The floor thumped as he crossed it. The door creaked, the chains rattled, and the padlock snicked, and she was left with the thump, thump, thump of the generator.

Creak, rattle, snick, and *thump, thump, thump.*

Until the fourth time.

It was important to keep track. She bent three fingers of her hand, holding the tips of her frigid fingers against the stiff pads of her palms, hoping she wouldn't relax when she slept; weak, cold, tired, hungry, scared. It was important not to lose track of time, not to lose count.

The fourth time was important.

She needed to be prepared.

As soon as he was gone she stared at the red light on the camera until all she could see was a circle of red. When it filled her vision she replayed the images of her capture, as if she could transmit them, record them on the camera as it recorded her, as if they might be found – clues to her disappearance, evidence to discount her death, and a trail that might lead to her location. She knew it was folly, that the images were trapped inside her head, and that the camera recorded only the dark outline of her captivity, no words or sounds. She glanced at the microphone on the floor beneath the camera – disconnected, discarded, redundant. No-one would hear her scream, not unless he wanted them to.

She thought about him, the elephant man, the rough skin of his hands on her arms, the twist of his fingers on her skin and the jerk of the greasy rope around her neck before he had brought her to the cabin. She had heard him hacking and chipping at the ice as she scratched and thumped at the inside of the car boot the day after she had been taken. She had fought him, but the second heavy blow to her head had dropped her onto the ice. He had bundled her into the boot, tied her hands and noosed her around the neck. He cursed her thumping, and she listened as he chipped at the ice.

When he finally opened the boot of the car, the fishing hole was the second thing she saw in the moonlight that night. The first was the barrel of the hunting rifle he pressed into her cheek. He tied one end of the rope around her neck to a hook he had dug in the ice, and then he forced her to strip, thrusting a piece of paper and a thick pencil into her hand as she shivered on the ice.

He told her what to write, gave her a metal plate to rest the paper on, and pointed the rifle at her. Petra's teeth chattered as her body temperature plummeted. She looked at the hole in the ice between each written word, until he slapped her and told her to be finished, quickly.

"I'm getting cold," he said. His breath was frosted in the fur around the rim of his hood. Her own breath cascaded down her body in puffs and clouds to the ice.

"Sign it and we can go."

Her signature, she realised, was her *affidavit*, notarized and authenticated by the gun. The hunter's law.

But she was not dead. The hole in the ice was not for her, at least not yet.

She added the Greenlandic spelling of her name to her signature.

Piitalaat.

If the suicide note kept her alive, then no matter what the physical or psychological cost, that one name would be enough to save her. *If*, of course, he saw it.

I need you, David, she thought, teeth chattering, as she gave the man the note and the pencil.

"Now get back in the boot," he said.

They were the last words she heard him speak before the cabin, but not the first.

The first time she saw him he was wearing a helmet. The visor was dark, impenetrable. She could barely hear him.

"Are you police?" he had asked, the Danish

words scratching through the visor.

"Yes."

"I need help. This way."

She had followed him from the store, past the post office and along the path below the colonial flagpole that reached high above the frozen surface of Uummannaq harbour. There were sledge dogs tethered along the path, and Petra had slowed, cautious all of a sudden, as her excitement about spending her first Christmas with Maratse was dulled by the sense that something was wrong about this man.

The body of a young man slumped on the sledge behind the snow scooter distracted her. She did a quick visual check of his condition, calling out to him, as she shook his shoulder and pressed her fingers to his neck to check for a pulse. His skin was warm and his pulse raced, but the young man, a teenager, was unresponsive.

"Has he taken something?" she said to the man in the helmet.

He responded with a flash of metal, striking a bar into the side of Petra's head.

She remembered the flap of a plastic tarpaulin covering her face, the bump of the sledge runners across the ice, and the medicinal breath of the teenager bound close to her body as they sped away from Uummannaq across the fjord.

Later, in the cabin, between the first and third changes of the camera card, Petra tried to recall what had happened, when they had been moved from the sledge to the car. Was the teenager moved with her? What had happened to him? He had never been in the cabin, had never been filmed, fed, or fettered – at least not with her. She believed he was dead, or perhaps there was another cabin, somewhere else on an island in the fjord.

He could be anywhere, she realised. How foolish it was to believe that a single name added to her signature might lead someone to find her.

"David," she said, forcing herself to stare at the camera.

She remembered their last night in the hotel in Berlin, his warm body pressed against hers. She could almost feel the heat, the light wisp of his beard on her neck, the rough skin of his hunter's hands, the calluses on his fisherman's fingers. He might have been a policeman once, but his body and mind were of the land, the rocks, the sea, and the ice. She closed her eyes, pictured his face, saw the gap between his teeth when he smiled, tried to measure the depths within his eyes – tried to read some of the pain he hid there.

David has survived somewhere and something like this. I can too.

There was a creak on the step.

Petra held her breath.

The rattle of the chain, each heavy link bumping over the iron rings was almost louder than the thump of her heart, but slower. Her heart beat in her chest like the rapid thump of the Arctic hare prepared for flight, or the Little Auk, wings spread, neck pinioned between finger and thumb, paralysed within the grasp of the hunter as he pulled it from the net.

She barely heard the snick in the lock, and the thump, thump of the generator could have been the blood pulsing in her ears.

This was the fourth time.

Petra's eyes widened, fixing on the man as he placed the dirty bowl of oatmeal on the floor, together with a glass of water. He turned his hood towards her for a second, and then he bent down to pick up the microphone from the floor. She held her breath as he attached it to the camera. And then she saw his eyes in the glow of the screen as he changed the card.

The analytical part of her brain determined that he must need more time to set up the microphone. He spent longer than usual behind the screen, and the light from the screen lit his eyes so brightly she thought they were burning; so intense was the energy that charged within them that his eyes might blister and pop from his face.

And then she understood why. She retreated across the dusty floor of the hunter's cabin, as far as the chain would allow, tugging the waistband of the jeans over her hips as she scooted backwards, away from the man, the camera, the microphone, and his intentions.

"David," she said. "David, help me."

"David?" The man's voice was muffled, his words funnelled through the hood. "Is that your policeman?"

Petra pressed her back against the wall, tucked her knees to her chest.

"David is not coming," the man said. "No-one is coming. It's just you and me." He smoothed his hand over the camera body as he took a step towards her. "And some friends," he said.

This was the fourth time.

She thought of the Auk, the hare, she thought of David. And then she stopped thinking. It was best not to think, not about the man, his friends, not even Maratse. If she was going to survive, she could not think.

Chapter 7

Gaba held tight to the handle above the passenger door as Simonsen bumped the police Toyota up and over the welt of ice on the ramp from the sea to the island. Miki hid a grin and the Commissioner smiled at him from the passenger seat. Gaba remembered that the Commissioner didn't get out much, as his job tied him to Nuuk and limited his movements to brief visits, courses, and the occasional meeting in Copenhagen. Driving across the sea ice and past the smaller villages and settlements on Greenland's coast was a welcome break from routine, despite the tragic reason for the visit. Simonsen slowed at the hotel but the Commissioner waved him on.

"You said we could see the body?"

"Now?"

"We fly tomorrow morning. If there's a link between the teenager's death and Sergeant Jensen, however tenuous, I want to know. Seeing the body might help."

"Okay," Simonsen said. He drove past the hotel and parked in front of the hospital.

Gaba could see the hotel dining room from the hospital parking area. There was a good view of the harbour, and he turned to scan the fishing boats frozen into the ice, and the sledges, snow scooters and dogs moored between the wooden hulls.

"What are you thinking, boss?" Miki asked as he joined Gaba.

"Petra wasn't taken from here, not without someone seeing her. Look." Gaba pointed. "The dock is wide open. There's plenty of activity, lots of lights." He nodded at the hotel. "There's a good view from there, and there's traffic on the road, people, taxis, sledges. Petra was too smart to just follow anyone. If she was taken, she must have been attacked somewhere, but not here."

"There's a road that runs around the harbour, past the post office. It's more secluded," Simonsen said. "It could have happened there."

"But you don't think she was taken, do you Simonsen?" the Commissioner asked.

"There are a lot of things I don't know. The note is compelling, but, suicide? I'll admit, it's out of character."

Simonsen lit a cigarette. "On the other hand, snatching a police officer is a little beyond what goes on around here. It's too elaborate a play for a local, too dangerous. The criminal element in Uummannaq is not so..."

"Clever?" Gaba said.

"I was going to say theatrical."

"And yet you've had a spate of *theatrics* of late," the Commissioner said. "Wouldn't you agree?"

"We've been busy," Simonsen said. "Ever since he arrived."

"By *he* you mean Maratse?"

"Yes."

"You're referring to the Tinka Winther case, and the *Ophelia*?"

"Two high profile cases within months of each other." Simonsen flicked his cigarette onto the ground, extinguishing it in the snow with the sole of his shoe. "It makes sense when you consider Maratse's past."

"I don't think that has anything to do with it, Chief."

"No? Maybe not, but it has *everything* to do with what kind of man he is."

"I think you should try to be more objective."

"I have tried. But this thing with Sergeant Jensen, it's just one more black mark against Maratse's name in my book. It makes sense when you put it in perspective." Simonsen caught Gaba's eye and then nodded for them to follow him. "The doctor is waiting," he said.

The storage room was too small for all of them to fit around the examination table. Miki volunteered to wait outside as Simonsen introduced them to Elena Bianchi, the doctor currently in charge of the hospital in Uummannaq.

"You're Italian?" the Commissioner said, as he shook her hand.

"Do you know how hard it is to find doctors willing to work this far north?"

Gaba smiled at the doctor's accented Danish.

"They won't even come on a short-term basis?"

"Sure they will, during the summer, once they have sold their practice and fancy a paid vacation in Greenland." Elena sighed. "I'm sorry," she said. "It's frustrating."

"We're pleased you're here," Simonsen said. "You've made a hit with the people in town and the settlements."

"Thank you, Torben," Elena said. "But, you're here to see Salik, right?"

"If you've got time?" the Commissioner said.

Elena nodded and pulled back the green paper sheet covering Salik's body.

"We don't do autopsies," she said. "And we don't have a morgue or cold storage. The Chief has kept us busy lately, so we have kept the bodies on ice from the fish factory, but..."

"This is Anton Erngsen's son," Simonsen said. "Anton runs the fish factory."

The Commissioner nodded, and pointed at the red welt around Salik's neck.

"It's possible he died from strangulation," Elena said. "But, he could also have bled out." She lifted Salik's wrists. The fingers were bent and bunched into a fist. She ran a gloved finger along the deep cuts on both of the teenager's forearms. "You can see he was bound." She shifted her grip to show the bruising around Salik's wrists. "And at the feet."

"Head, hands, and feet," Gaba said.

"That's right." Elena lowered Salik's arms to the table. She smoothed her hand across the skin and patted the back of his hand. Softly, quickly, but long enough for the men to pause and wait for her to speak. "It's possible he was pulled in this position."

"Pulled?" the Commissioner asked.

"I mean *stretched*. Sometimes I forget the correct word."

The Commissioner smiled. "It's not a problem. Tell me more."

"I think he was stretched in at least two directions. There is bruising on the tops of his feet, as if a rope or chain pressed into his skin, and he couldn't move."

"That would require space," Gaba said. "Outside, with a scooter perhaps?"

"Possibly."

"Which meant the killer had time, and wasn't worried about being seen." Gaba looked at Simonsen. "This happened deeper in the fjord."

"That's likely, but we found the body at the corner of Salliaruseq, the big island just over there, seven kilometres from here. The body was dumped close to the ice road to Saattut. We were meant to find it. Just like we were meant to find Sergeant Jensen's note."

"They have to be related," Gaba said.

Elena waited for Gaba to finish.

"Suicide is just as common here as it is in Nuuk," she said.

"You didn't know Petra."

"Take it easy, Gaba," the Commissioner said. He pointed at a clipboard hanging from the end of the examination table. "What are they?"

"Photos," Elena said. "Of his back."

The Commissioner picked up the clipboard and leafed through the photos.

"These are fish hooks?"

"Yes."

"And threads?"

"Different colours. All of them. The hooks were attached to his body, and then sealed into his skin with a blowtorch. Those are burn marks, not blood, you can see in the photos."

Gaba studied the photos as the Commissioner turned the clipboard towards him.

"And these photos?" he asked. "What's that on the inside of his hands?"

"Inside his fingers." Elena lifted one of Salik's arms and prised the fingers from his palms, straightening them and exposing black bands between the joints in his fingers. "I thought they were bruises or burns at first," she said. "As if he had held something."

"They're tattoos," Gaba said, as he pressed his face closer to Salik's hand. "Stick and poke."

"What's that?" the Commissioner asked.

"A needle or something sharp, poking ink beneath the surface. It's not a tattoo machine."

"It's rough work. Amateurish," Elena said, as she showed Gaba the boy's other hand. "But all of the spaces between the joints are inked. Three on each finger, two on each thumb."

"Did you know him?" Gaba asked Simonsen.

"Reasonably well," he said. "Mostly through his father."

"Anything to suggest he was into something?"

"No more than any of the teenagers here. He drank too much. He smoked and had tried sniffing at some point in his past."

"Sex?"

"What about it?"

"If he was like the other teens in town..."

"You think this is sexually motivated?"

Gaba turned to the Commissioner. "This is pretty weird, sir. The hooks. The coloured threads. I don't know about the bands on his fingers, but something was going on with this kid."

"I agree."

"I don't suppose I am breaking patient confidentiality now that he is dead," Elena said. "But Salik came to see me twice this year. In the summer he complained of sores on his penis. He tested positive for syphilis. There has been a small surge in cases around here recently."

"Also in Nuuk," the Commissioner said. "And the second time?"

"Was when we did a test for tuberculosis, of the

whole town. Salik tested positive for latent TB. He was not sick and he showed no symptoms. It's possible that if his immune system was weakened he might develop the disease."

"Weak with syphilis, for example?"

"We treated him for that. It was in the early stages. But if he was sexually active, of course, he could be exposed again." She tapped the clipboard in the Commissioner's hand. "The lab technician is at home with a migraine, and we're waiting on the results of the tests."

"Thank you, doctor," the Commissioner said, and handed her the clipboard. He gestured for Simonsen and Gaba to follow him into the corridor. "I'm leaving Miki here," he said to Simonsen. "Gaba will brief him about Salik."

"Is he reporting back to you?" Simonsen asked.

"He's assisting you, and keeping Gaba and me in the loop, yes."

"I can do that."

"I know you can, Chief, but you're stretched pretty thin. Miki is here to help. Use him," he said. "Now, before you take us to the hotel, tell me who might have done something like this, however unlikely, however *theatrical*."

Simonsen looked at the Commissioner. "You're taking Gaba back with you?"

"Yes."

"Because if we're trying to link the two..."

"Just say it, Simonsen," Gaba said.

"Easy now," he said. "I heard you and Petra were a couple."

"That was a while ago."

"What I don't need right now is for Gaba to go

off the rails," Simonsen said. He looked at the Commissioner. "Everyone knows Gaba Alatak. He's your pit-bull."

"Sergeant Alatak leads the SRU, Chief. I think you should choose your next words carefully. This is an emotional time. We have just buried a colleague. It is in everyone's interest to bring this investigation to a satisfactory close. It won't bring Sergeant Jensen back, but it might help all of us, and those who cared about her, to move on. Sergeant Alatak is responsible for his actions, but he's under my command, as are you, Chief. So, tell us what you know, or what you are thinking, and we can move on with the investigation."

Simonsen glanced at Gaba.

"Alright," Simonsen said. "There's one man, a Dane, who I would like to talk to about Sergeant Jensen's disappearance, and the murder of Salik Erngsen."

"His name?" Gaba asked.

"Aksel Stein," Simonsen said. "There's just one problem, no-one has seen him for over a week. But if we find him, we might find some answers. That's where I would start, after we've talked with Salik's parents." Simonsen sighed. "That's not going to be easy."

Tallimanngorneq

FRIDAY

Chapter 8

The brief period of grey twilight had passed, dragging the memory of Petra Jensen's funeral into the winter night. A fresh wind teased at the light layer of new snow that had fallen since Maratse stood beside Petra's grave, twisting the snowflakes in front of the runners of his sledge as he encouraged the small Greenlandic sledge dog, Tinka, to lead the team with gentle snaps of the whip on the ice. The sledge creaked past the corner of Salliaruseq, past the spot where they had found the body of the teenager, Salik, and on to the fishing hole in the ice. Maratse paused there for an hour, scouring the surface of the ice with a torch, and resisting the temptation to reel in the long line one more time. The crime scene, if it could be called that, was clean, with no further evidence of Petra having been there. But a closer inspection of the wooden legs supporting the drum of fishing line revealed a tiny purple thread of cotton beneath a splinter of wood. It twisted in the light wind. Maratse teased it free, examined it for a moment and then wrapped it around his finger before stuffing his hand back inside his sealskin mittens.

Buuti had sewn the mittens for Karl the previous winter, just as she had sewn each of the items that Maratse wore above his thermal layers. The white cotton anorak he wore above the sealskin top, the polar bear skin trousers, even the *kamikker* he wore on his feet – it was all Buuti's work, all white. With the hood drawn above the white silk ski mask Karl had tucked into the pockets of Maratse's anorak, the only item not handmade. From a distance, Maratse was practically invisible, a ghost on the ice.

The dog team stirred as he walked back to the sledge. They watched as Maratse drifted the torchlight across the frozen surface of the sea, pausing at the tyre tracks furrowed into the ice and leading to the settlement of Saattut. If Petra had been here, if she had been brought by car, then the car must have stopped in the tracks – there was no other sign – about one hundred metres from the fishing hole, a long way to walk with no clothes. If she had been here. If *he* had brought her here at all.

Maratse had a name for *him*. Danielsen had given it to him earlier in the month. There had been a confrontation with an older Dane driving a snow scooter – the man had nearly run over Sisse's daughter, Nanna. According to Danielsen, the man, Aksel Stein, had a history of abuse. His behaviour that day put him at the top of Maratse's list. Aksel's profile – a reclusive man with an attitude and a history of violence – made up for the apparent lack of motive, but Maratse needed a place to start. He took a last look at the ice and walked back to the sledge. At a soft clap from Maratse, Tinka tightened the traces and the team lurched into motion, the sledge grated across the ice to one side of the car tracks towards Saattut.

Saattut was a little over twenty kilometres northeast of the island of Uummannaq. Half an hour by car, perhaps twice that by sledge. Maratse used the time to plan his next move. He knew he was looking for a remote cabin – the one Aksel supposedly occupied throughout the year. One of Saattut's two hundred inhabitants knew where that was, and one of them was going to tell Maratse before the dawn of another dark day in December. Maratse barely felt the wind through the mask covering his face, nor did it penetrate the bearskin trousers, or the thick sealskin covering his upper body, but he was cold, chilled from his stomach at the thought of yet another day that Petra was in danger. If he had revealed his face to any observer they would have seen that chill twist into a fierce determination, a dangerous motivation, and one that held little regard for those obstructing his investigation.

Maratse was on the trail of a monster. A monster who would breach the quiet restraints for which Maratse was known, in order to save the one he loved. He knew now that it was love, and there was nothing he wouldn't do if someone he loved was threatened or in danger. He pulled the rifle from the scabbard slung from the sledge upright and chambered a bullet in the barrel. Tinka flicked her head to look at him as the metal snicked and clicked in the darkness.

"Go on now," he said.

The sledge lurched and creaked as Tinka picked up speed and the team of eight sledge dogs behind her increased the pace. Maratse would have to slow them before the settlement, and, as the lights above the tiny harbour dock grew stronger, he rested the rifle in his lap and used the whip to drive the team to the right of the settlement. He stopped them by a drift of snow half a kilometre from the tip of Saattut island. Maratse dug a loop in the ice and anchored the team. He heard them settle on the snow as he slung the rifle over his shoulder and walked towards the island.

The Christmas stars shone from the windows, casting soft red and orange lights on the snow outside the brightly painted houses. The people of Saattut were indoors, but the local dogs stirred as he whispered past them, their chains rattling across the exposed rock at Maratse's ghost-like image. He stopped by the tiny school building, scanned the neighbouring houses, tilting his head to one side at the sound of seventies rock music thumping through the thin walls of a blue house close to the harbour building. Maratse walked towards it.

He caught a whiff of herbed smoke and slowed at the sight of two men, younger than Maratse, drinking and smoking outside the house. He watched them for a moment, gauging how much they had had to drink, how much they had smoked, with the eye of a policeman used to weekend shifts in the Arctic. If he had to go house-to-house, if he had to rouse the whole settlement, then that is what he would do. But the smell of hashish, the loud music, and the raucous nature of the party indicated that the people in this house might have the answers he needed. Like attracts like, and Aksel, Maratse determined, had more in common with the people partying in the house, than the quiet families in the rest of the settlement.

Maratse leaned his rifle against a large fishing box beneath a drying rack to the right of the house. He tucked the mittens inside the chest pockets of his anorak, unwinding the purple thread from his finger and slipping it inside one of the mittens. He removed his anorak and the sealskin, draping them over the box, before he pushed the sleeves of his thermal top further up his arms.

Then he took a breath and walked towards the house.

"Hey, look," said the shorter of the two men

smoking by the front door. "It's *Julemanden.*" He passed the joint to his friend and patted the front of his black hoodie. "He needs to eat more."

"*Aap,*" said the other man. "He's too thin to be Father Christmas."

Maratse stopped in front of the man in the hoodie.

"Is this your house?"

"Who wants to know?"

"I want to know. Do you live here?"

"*Imaqa.* Maybe. Why?"

"I'm looking for someone."

The man slapped his friend on the arm. "He's looking for someone." He slipped his hand inside the pocket at the front of his hoodie and pulled out a thin knife. "Are you police?"

Maratse shrugged. "I'm retired."

"Pigs don't retire," the man said. He nodded at his friend and thrust the knife towards Maratse's face.

Maratse moved to one side and then stepped towards the man, wrapping his arm around the man's knife arm, and dropping him to the ground with a swift kick to the knee. He gripped the man's chin and lifted his head.

"Drop the knife."

"Piss off," the man said, with a glance at his friend.

Maratse saw the second man flick his joint into the snow and raise his fist. He threw a punch at Maratse, catching him on the shoulder as Maratse turned and twisted the man with the knife onto the snow in front of his friend. Maratse ducked beneath a second swing, grabbed the man's arm and pulled him over the man sprawled on the snow. When both men were on the ground, Maratse stepped around them and walked across the snow to the house.

The music thumped through the walls and vibrated through the door handle as Maratse turned it and stepped inside. Maratse had been called to more than one *after party* in his career. He ignored the couple having sex on the sofa and crossed the floor to the stereo. Maratse glanced at a young woman sprawled in an armchair, a triangle of alcohol stained the front of her top. She shrieked when he pulled the stereo plug from the socket and the music stopped, just as the two men from outside the house lurched through the door, snow scattering from their shoes as they ran towards Maratse.

"He's police," said the man with the knife.

"I'm not here for you," Maratse said. "Just listen for a moment."

The two men from outside drifted to the walls, one on each side of Maratse. The woman in the armchair slid off the cushions and onto the floor, while the couple having sex stopped and stared. Maratse looked at the two young men flanking him, and pointed at the man with the knife.

"I'm looking for Aksel Stein," he said.

"Aksel?"

"*Iiji.*"

The man on the sofa climbed off the woman beneath him and pulled up his jeans. He wobbled as he tightened his belt, and then waved at the two young men to stand still.

"Why?" he said.

"That's my business," Maratse said. "There's a cabin that Aksel uses. Do you know where it is?"

"There are lots of cabins," the man said.

"And he uses one of them."

"*Aap*, from time to time. When he's not here."

"What?"

"This is Aksel's house. He only goes to the cabin when he is going to get drunk."

"He lives here?"

"*Aap.*"

"And all of you live here too?"

"*Naamik*," the man said. "Just me."

"And who are you?"

"I'm Aksel's son."

Maratse took a moment to look around the room. The few pictures in the lounge hung at odd angles, tilted by the bass and the drums beating through the walls. The picture closest to Maratse showed an older Dane with a young Greenlandic woman. He looked at Aksel's son and pointed at the picture.

"My mother," the man said.

"She doesn't live here?"

The man shook his head.

"Where's the cabin?"

"South of here. In the fjord."

"You can show me on a map?"

"*Aap*. But it won't help."

"Why not?"

"He's not there. I haven't seen him for a week."

It made sense that Aksel would be missing, that no-one would know where he was. But, empty or not, Maratse had to see Aksel's cabin. He reached into a pocket sewn inside the leg of the bearskin trousers and pulled out Petra's note together with the stub of a pencil. He pressed the note against the wall and drew a rough map of the fjord on the back of it.

"You," he said and pointed at Aksel's son. "Show

me where the cabin is. The rest of you can leave."
Maratse glared at the two young men he had fought
with. "Leave or I'll call the police." He waited as they
drifted out of the room and then gestured for Aksel's
son to walk over to him. "I don't have time to waste.
Show me where the cabin is."

Chapter 9

The snow settled on the lid of the cardboard box in Qitu's hands as he stepped off the bus on *Aqqusinersuaq*, Nuuk's main street. He walked north past Hotel Hans Egede and east along *Kongevej*, until he reached a low building next to the CrossFit gym. He rested the box on a railing as he fished the keys from his jacket pocket. Once inside, Qitu pushed the box onto a large empty desk and removed the satchel slung over his shoulder. He searched for a plug socket, powered up his *MacBook* and investigated the kitchen. Palu had promised that it would be fully stocked, but the fridge was mouldy, and the cord for the coffee machine was frayed, almost severed, just like Qitu's contract with *Sermitsiaq*.

"You're crazy," his boss had said the day after Qitu's meeting with Palu and the girl.

"I know."

"Then why?"

Qitu remembered shrugging and his now former boss shaking his head. There was nothing more to say. He couldn't explain why he was prepared to swap a promising position as journalist with Greenland's leading newspaper for an unknown future with a start-up media group, but something about Tertu's story intrigued him. It felt more important than reporting the regular news and he realised that ever since working on the Tinka Winther story, he had been longing for a similar story, one that would shake its readers and maybe even make a difference.

The sentimentality and sudden righteousness made him laugh, and he felt the vibration of his voice through the walls around the tiny kitchen. But without coffee, any grand plans Qitu had for a big story would grind to a halt. He checked his calendar on his phone and decided he had plenty of time to visit the store before Tertu arrived. *If* she arrived. While he didn't doubt she had a story to tell, he did wonder if she was willing to tell it. Qitu locked the door on the way out and turned his collar up as the snow swirled about the streets of Nuuk.

Thoughts of a related story drifted through Qitu's mind as he walked towards the town centre. A year ago he had been assigned to research a story about homosexuality in Greenland. He remembered an interview he had arranged with the church. The official comment from the Bishop's office at the time had been one of pity for the gay people of Greenland. Qitu had pressed for a deeper explanation but had left the interview with little more than a promise that the Lutheran Church of Greenland was interested in the spiritual welfare of all the people of Greenland.

"But it's only the gays you pity, isn't that right?" Qitu had asked.

The interview had ended with no further comment, and the quote had been removed in the final edit of the article.

Nuuk was often considered to be a provincial town, a fact that could be seen and heard in the attitudes of many of its residents, both Greenlandic and Danish. The acceptance of alternative lifestyles was more on a par with a small town in Denmark, with some enlightened views and a good measure of ignorance and incomprehension. But Nuuk was a city with all the trappings of an Arctic capital, with grander plans than the size of its population might warrant. To be pitied might even be the enviable alternative to being shunned or ignored. Qitu understood that for a lot of gay men in Greenland, sex and sexuality was linked to alcohol – strong spirits that set them free.

The idea of an underground network for sex suggested something else, and it intrigued him. Greenland is a vast country with great distances between the towns, villages, and settlements. Flying is expensive; there are no roads connecting the communities, and local travel meant a boat in the summer, and a snow scooter, car or even a sledge in the winter. And that is only if the ice is strong enough, if it came at all. A network that provided sex for alternative tastes, that didn't rely on alcohol and after parties would also be expensive and no doubt lucrative for those who controlled it.

Qitu stopped at the door to *Brugsen*, glancing at the drunks clumped on either side of the street. There were plenty of people ripe for exploitation in Greenland. If he could write something that might make a difference, that might change the status quo, then he considered that his duty. The thought buoyed him through the entrance of the store and along the aisles as he searched for coffee.

A hand on Qitu's arm made him turn. He smiled when he recognised an older colleague, one of the Danes who had taken him under his wing when Qitu was just starting out as a journalist. He focused on Jerrik Poulsen's mouth as he spoke.

"You've left *Sermitsiaq*?" he asked.

"Yes."

"Where are you working now?"

"Just off *Kongevej*. Palu hired me to work for Nuuk Media Group. This is my first day."

"Palu Didriksen?"

Qitu nodded.

"That's a curious move." Jerrik frowned as he looked at Qitu. "Everything alright?"

"Yes."

"When did you move?"

"I picked up my things last night."

"Then you haven't heard about the police Sergeant who committed suicide?"

"Who?"

"A woman." Jerrik paused. "A Danish surname. Jensen, I think."

"Petra Jensen?"

"That's the one. Did you know her?"

Qitu gripped the shelf on his left as he processed the news. He liked Petra, and he liked her friend, the retired Constable.

"Maratse," he said.

"What's that?"

"She had a friend called Maratse. This will hit him hard."

"That's not all. They found a body the same day they discovered the Sergeant's clothes and a note."

"What body?"

Jerrik reached into his shopping basket. "This one," he said and handed Qitu a copy of *Sermitsiaq*. "There's not much information yet, but they found the body of a young man, still in his teens. The police have yet to comment; a taxi driver found the boy. He mentioned something about fish hooks and strange markings on the boy's hands." Jerrik took the paper when Qitu was finished with it. "I hope the job with Palu works out, because I think you just missed out on a good story. We haven't heard the last of this, that's for sure." Jerrik tossed the paper into his basket. "Look after yourself, Qitu. Call me if you need anything."

Qitu nodded as Jerrik shook his hand. He waited until the man was gone and then pulled out his phone, unlocking it and searching through his contacts for Maratse's number. He paused before sending a message. What could he possibly write? He settled on a short message of condolence and the promise to help if Maratse needed anything. He stared at the screen for a second, pressed the icon to send the message, and then slipped the phone into his pocket. Qitu added a paper to his basket and went to the checkout, pausing at the shop door to read the story one more time before walking back to his office.

Qitu barely noticed the snow as he considered the details of the article, the speculation, and the reluctance of the police to comment at this time. *Out of respect for the family*, Qitu mused as he fumbled with the keys in his pocket. A shock of pink hair made him start as he pulled out his keys. The tusks, he noticed, were gone, replaced with flat black squares. They were unremarkable and he wondered if she was toning down her appearance, trying to blend in. Then he glanced at her hair. *Not yet*, he thought.

"You're early," he said, as he unlocked the door.

Tertu said nothing. She followed him inside and found a seat in his office.

"Do you want coffee?" Qitu tossed the newspaper onto the desk and waited for Tertu to speak. "I'll make a pot," he said, and walked into the kitchen.

Qitu stared at the cord of the coffee machine as the water heated and started to percolate through the coffee grounds. He didn't know if his sense of smell compensated for his hearing difficulties, but the smell of coffee always calmed him. He waited until the jug was full and poured two mugs, the last drips of water spat and sizzled on the hot plate as he removed the jug. Tertu was standing at the back of the office when he put the mugs on the desk, arms wrapped around her body, shoulders trembling.

"Tertu?"

Qitu caught her eye and followed her gaze to the newspaper on the desk. It was open at page two, the continuation of the story from the front page. Qitu turned the paper towards him and looked at Tertu.

"Did you know Salik Erngsen?" he asked.

She shook her head. He watched as she slipped her hands slowly out of the sleeves of her hoodie and turned her palms towards him. She tapped the two spaces on her finger and nodded at the paper on the desk.

"But you knew *of* him?"

Tertu nodded.

"He's free now," she said. "That's his reward."

"You think he's connected? To your story?"

"*Aap.*"

"But are you sure? You said you don't know him."

Tertu walked back to the desk and sat down. Qitu handed her a mug of coffee and she warmed her hands around it. He stared at the Aleut markings tattooed into her fingers and pictured the darker bands poked into her skin on the other side.

"He liked my Aleut tattoos," she said, and lifted her fingers. "That's what gave him the idea to mark people." Tertu turned her palm towards Qitu. "And that," she said, and pointed at the newspaper.

"We need to be sure," Qitu said. "If Salik is linked to your story."

"Then he is the first one to die."

"That we know of."

Qitu sat on the desk and considered Salik's place in Tertu's story. If he could prove there was a connection, then he had the foundations of an investigation. Travel to Uummannaq was expensive, but if he could confirm the link then he could justify the expense, and discover just how deep the Nuuk Media Group's pockets really were. He needed help, someone in the area.

"Maratse," he said.

"Who?"

"He's a friend. A retired policeman. He lives in the area. He might be able to help us."

"Then call him," Tertu said.

"I can't." Qitu sighed.

"Why not?"

"His friend just committed suicide. It's too soon."

"Too soon?" Tertu gripped the mug until her fingers turned white. "Salik is already dead. If I'm found, then I'll be next."

"We don't know that. In fact," Qitu said, "I don't know anything. That's why you're here today, so I can find out more."

"Salik's death changes everything," she said. "You have to call your friend."

Friend, Qitu thought as he looked at Tertu. He knew Maratse only a little more than he knew the young woman sitting in front of him. But what he knew about him, what he had observed and discovered when working with him, was Maratse's moral centre – he would do the right thing, selflessly, if asked, perhaps even in his time of grief, and especially if he knew someone's life was in danger. Qitu took out his phone, opened his messages and stared at the new thread he had started less than an hour ago. It was absurd, heartless, but necessary. He glanced at Tertu, nodded once, and started typing. Time would tell if Maratse could help, if he even saw the message. Qitu looked at the girl once more and wondered how much time she had left.

Chapter 10

"I need you to stay here and mind the shop," Simonsen said, as he stopped Miki at the door to the police station. He pointed at the counter. "Any problems give us a call. We'll be at the Erngsen's house."

"The Commissioner said I was to be a part of the investigation."

"I heard him. But I also heard him say you were working on Sergeant Jensen's case."

"The two could be connected."

"Then why don't you use your superior policing skills and find out. Or don't they teach you how to do that in the SRU?"

Miki bit back a laugh and stared at Uummannaq's Chief of Police.

"Do you want to say something, Constable?"

"*Naamik.*"

"Because it looks like you do."

"I've got nothing to say, Chief."

Simonsen tapped a cigarette out of the packet and stuck it between his lips. He fiddled with his lighter as he looked at the young police officer.

"You know what I think?"

"What's that?"

"I think Greenland is too small for SRU. I think local policing is the key and that the likes of you and your boss..."

"Sergeant Alatak."

"The one with the muscles and the swagger, that's right. He belongs in America, not here."

"But you need us once in a while, Chief."

"That's debatable." Simonsen nodded at the

counter. "Mind the shop, and stay out of my office."

"Yes, sir."

Simonsen grunted and walked out of the police station. He lit his cigarette and waved to Danielsen that he was ready. He opened the passenger door of the police car and climbed in, winding the window down an inch to allow the smoke from his cigarette to drift out of the car into the cold, dark night.

"Anton Erngsen will want to know when his son's body will be released," Simonsen said. "But I want you to wait before you tell him. As soon as he knows that he'll be thinking of the service and the funeral. We need to interview him first."

"Interview?"

"Questions." Simonsen flicked his cigarette out of the window. "His wife, Oline, will be there. If Anton offers us a coffee, I want you to go into the kitchen with her. Talk with her. I can't, her Danish isn't so good."

"Salik is their only son," Danielsen said, as he slowed for a hunter pushing a sledge with a team of dogs to the ice. Danielsen waved at him.

"I know," Simonsen said. "Just be gentle, and see if you can look at Salik's computer or his phone."

Danielsen nodded and they drove the rest of the way in silence.

The front of the house was dark when they pulled up outside it. Simonsen knocked on the door as Danielsen peered inside the kitchen window. It took three more knocks before Anton opened the door and invited them inside.

"Oline is still in bed," he said. "Do you want coffee?"

Simonsen nodded for Danielsen to wait in the

lounge. He followed Anton into the kitchen. The sink was full of dishes and ash flowed from a saucer on the kitchen table. Simonsen picked up an empty beer bottle from the counter and slipped it into the plastic crate of empties by the back door.

"When can we see Salik?" Anton asked, as he filled the kettle with water.

"We're waiting to hear from the hospital. If they don't call before we leave, I'll call them."

"Okay."

Simonsen pulled out a chair and sat at the table. Anton lit a cigarette and sat opposite him.

"I usually smoke outside," he said, and shrugged.

"That's okay."

The kettle boiled and Anton poured three cups of coffee. His cigarette burned on the table. Simonsen picked it up and placed it on the saucer.

"Aqqa," Anton called out. He handed Danielsen a coffee as the young Constable came into the kitchen and put the other two cups on the table.

"Does Salik have a computer?" Simonsen asked.

Anton raised his eyebrows, *yes*.

"Does it have a password?"

"Maybe. I don't know."

"Can I have a look at it?" Danielsen asked.

"It's in his room. Down there," Anton said.

Danielsen nodded at Simonsen and slipped out of the kitchen. Anton watched him leave. The cigarette burned in the saucer as the two men drank their coffee.

"You know I need to ask some questions, Anton."

"*Aap.*"

"Are you ready?"

"Sure." Anton shrugged.

"When did you last see Salik?"

"*Marlunngorneq*," he said. "Tuesday."

"Last week?"

"*Aap.*"

"Where was he?" Simonsen waited as Anton lit another cigarette. It burned between his fingers, the smoke mixing with more from the cigarette still burning in the saucer. "Was he with friends?"

"Maybe."

"Who are his friends?"

"Natsi."

"Natsi Hermansen?"

"And Aaju."

"I don't know him."

"Aaju Imiina. He lives up on *Juaarsip Aqqutaa*. The blue house, next to the teacher's house."

"Where's Aaju from?"

"Nuuk, maybe."

"And it was just the two of them, and Salik?"

Anton finished his coffee and stubbed his cigarette out in the saucer. Simonsen looked through the kitchen door and listened to the sound of Danielsen typing on a keyboard. He pulled out his notebook and made a note of the two names.

"Anyone else? Any girls?"

"Pah," Anton said. "No girls for Salik."

"No?"

"You never heard what they say about my son?"

Simonsen had heard the stories. It was hard to be different in a town with just over two thousand people. He remembered when Salik was a happy young teenager, before he became moody and withdrawn in his last year at school. Simonsen lost touch with him then as Salik seemed to vanish. He looked at the names on the list. Aaju was a new one, but Simonsen knew Natsi. The kids called him *Nasty*. Simonsen found out why the first time he put him in jail for the night to sober up. But whether it was Natsi's hygiene, language or sexual preferences that earned him the nickname, Simonsen didn't know. Unfortunately, given that Natsi was the name at the top of Simonsen's list, he realised he might yet find out.

"No-one else?" Simonsen asked. "What about older men? A Dane perhaps."

"When Salik went fishing, sometimes he was gone for a week," Anton said. "Sometimes two weeks. I asked him why he never went fishing with me. Why he never spent time with me? He said he didn't like fishing. So, I asked him why he did something he didn't like. He said it was a job." Anton stared at Simonsen. "I never saw him get on a boat, or drive out to a fishing hole. He always wore jeans. He never had any working gloves. Not even a knife." Anton pointed at his jacket hanging by the kitchen door. "I have a knife. I have gloves." He paused. "You know what I think?"

"What's that?"

"I don't think my son was a fisherman."

"No, Anton, I don't think he was either."

Danielsen knocked softly on the door frame and nodded for Simonsen to come with him. Anton lit another cigarette and they left him in the kitchen.

"In here," Danielsen said.

He led Simonsen into Salik's room. Danielsen pulled out the chair in front of the computer and waited for the Chief to sit down. Simonsen took a moment to look at the pop posters tacked to the walls and the rumpled sheets of Salik's bed. He wrinkled his nose at the smell and Danielsen shrugged.

"It smells of teenager," he said. "You'll get used to it."

"I don't think I want to."

Danielsen leaned around Simonsen and used the computer mouse to click on the screen and open a series of photographs. Each photo was dark and blurry. There were figures in the background, but the eyes were red, the features grainy. Danielsen tapped the screen on each of the photos. The flash had caught the skin of fingers too close to the lens, giving each photo a white glare in the left corner of the image that obscured the background.

"Do you see it?"

"See what?"

"The threads wrapped around the fingers," Danielsen said. "Here." He tapped one of the photos. "And here. Purple and green. This one," he said, as he clicked through two more photos, "is blue."

"Threads, like the ones from the hooks."

"And something else." Danielsen clicked back to the first photo. He tapped the screen. "Look there. In the corner of the photo."

"Is that shadow or..."

"It could be shadow. But I think it is a black band on the inside of his fingers."

"Whose? Salik's?"

"Maybe." Danielsen took a step back. "I can't tell."

"But if it is Salik. Who are they?" Simonsen pointed at the two men in their early twenties in the background. He showed Danielsen the list in his notebook.

"That's *Nasty*," Danielsen said and tapped the image of the man on the left. "He has an afro wig. I've seen him wear it around town."

"And him?" Simonsen pointed at the man on the right. "Is that Aaju?"

"Who's Aaju?"

"I don't know. But he's staying on *Juaarsip*."

Simonsen clicked through the images to the last one in the folder. He fiddled with the mouse and then leaned back as Danielsen enlarged the image. A third figure with long black hair was lost in the shadow of the corner of the room. The same room as the other photos, but a different time – the light outside the window was grey, not black, and the mountains were just visible.

"Where is this taken?" Simonsen said.

Danielsen zoomed in on the window in the centre of the photograph. He stared at it for a minute and then shook his head.

"I don't recognise it."

"And the one with the long hair? Is that a boy or a girl?"

"I don't know."

"*Niviarsiaq*," said a voice from the door.

Simonsen turned to see Oline Erngsen standing in the corridor outside Salik's room. Her finger trembled as she pointed at the computer screen.

"*Niviarsiaq*," she said. "A girl."

"Do you know her name?" Simonsen asked.

Oline shook her head and slid away from the door.

"We need the photos," Simonsen said, as he stood up.

"How? I don't have a USB drive."

Simonsen shrugged. "Take the computer."

"The whole thing?"

"Yes," he said and walked out of the room.

Oline reached for a bottle of beer from the crate on the floor, checking each one to see if it was empty. Simonsen took her arm and pulled her gently to the kitchen table. Anton stared at his wife.

"You can arrange to have Salik moved to the chapel," he said. "Call me if there is anything you remember. Anything at all."

"Are you going to find out who killed our son?" Anton asked.

"I'm going to try," he said.

Simonsen nodded goodbye and left the kitchen. He met Danielsen in the hall and opened the front door as the Constable carried the computer to the rear of the police car.

"Where to, boss?" Danielsen asked, as he opened the driver's door.

Simonsen held up his finger for Danielsen to wait, as he pressed his mobile to his ear. His breath misted in front of him, beading on the front of his jacket in a fine sheen of ice.

"Miki? Take a taxi and meet us at *Juaarsip Aqqutaa*," Simonsen said. He walked around the car and opened the passenger door. "Wait. You still there? Bring the vests and a rifle from the cabinet."

Danielsen grinned as Simonsen closed the door.

"What is it, Aqqa?"

"You told Miki to bring the vests and a gun?"

"So?"

"He's SRU. You told him this morning that we didn't need him."

"You heard that?"

"*Aap.*"

"Things change, Constable." He sighed as Danielsen laughed. "Just shut up and drive."

Arfininngorneq

SATURDAY

Chapter 11

Danielsen parked alongside the taxi on the road below *Juaarsip Aqqutaa.* There were three twin houses on the rocks above them. The houses shared twenty wooden steps to the decks at the front of each twin house. Simonsen pointed at the rocks below Natsi's house as Danielsen fastened the ballistic vest over his police sweater and Miki checked the rifle.

"We know Natsi is in Uummannaq," Simonsen said. "And at this time of day he's probably in bed. He won't be up before late afternoon."

"Anyone else inside?" Miki asked.

"Natsi's sister, maybe. And maybe our mystery man Aaju Imiina. He could be on a visit from Nuuk."

Miki nodded and pointed at the rocks behind the house.

"If they run then they will come out the back window. There's no back door on these types of houses. I'll wait there and you flush them out."

Simonsen turned at the sound of Danielsen repositioning the broad Velcro tabs on his vest. He rapped his knuckles on the younger man's chest.

"Wipe that smile off your face, Aqqa."

"Chief?"

"I can see it in your eyes. You're excited, and Miki is talking you up. We're picking up two young men, that's all. They're not bank robbers."

"Then why the vests?"

Simonsen tucked his thumbs inside his belt and looked at Danielsen. "Because," he said, "I don't know Aaju, and I don't like surprises." He threw his jacket onto the back seat of the car and took a vest from Miki. Simonsen nodded at the taxi driver as he tightened the straps at the sides. "The sooner we get a second vehicle the better," he said. "Danielsen, pay Taavi and be sure to get a receipt."

Miki slung the rifle over his shoulder and looked up at the houses. Just like all the houses in the smaller villages and settlements in Greenland, the water and electricity pipes were laid above ground. Like stiff snakes in metal collars, they connected each house to the mains. Miki would have to crawl over them as he worked his way over the snow and ice to the back of the house. The street lights lit the front, but there was a dark patch of shadow beneath the bedroom window.

Miki nodded towards the shadows, "I'll be there."

"Miki, wait," Simonsen said.

"*Aap?*"

"No heroics, okay?"

"With respect, Chief, you seem to have some issues you need to work through."

"Issues? What I have is problems, the kind that we never used to have here. Ever since Maratse turned up, we have had more violent crime in one year than I can remember in the twenty years I have been in Uummannaq. This is the second time this year you have been here, Miki, and I don't like it."

"I'll do my job, Chief."

"I don't doubt it, I just don't like that you have to. Added to that," he said, as Danielsen approached them, "you're a bad influence on him." He gestured towards Danielsen. "We'll give you two minutes before we start walking around the front."

Simonsen resisted the urge to smoke as he watched Miki move into position. Once the SRU Constable from Nuuk waved that he was ready,

Simonsen tapped Danielsen on the shoulder and walked to the foot of the stairs leading to the houses on *Juaarsip Aqqutaa*. They passed the first house and continued on to the first step below Natsi's house. The kitchen light shone through the window and lit the deck outside. Unlike the other houses in Uummannaq, there were no Christmas stars in the windows, and little to suggest that the occupants had much to get excited about in the holiday period.

Simonsen knew Natsi and many others like him. Out of work, struggling with a tough family background, and burying all of that beneath a tough facade and alcohol binges that lasted from Wednesday to Monday every week. Simonsen looked at his watch. It was Saturday. He nodded at the kitchen window and listened as the snow on the deck crunched beneath Danielsen's boots. At a shrug from the Constable, Simonsen knocked on the door.

"Natsi? It's Simonsen. Open the door."

They waited in anticipation of some movement inside, and the vibration common in houses built on thick wooden foundations and bolted to the rocks.

"Natsi?"

Simonsen turned the door handle and opened the door slowly. Danielsen peered around it and nodded that it was clear. Simonsen was the first inside. He checked the bathroom on the immediate left as Danielsen walked into the kitchen.

"Natsi?" Danielsen said. "It's the police."

They stopped at the sound of something heavy falling onto the floor in the living room, on the other side of the kitchen door. Simonsen tapped Danielsen's shoulder and followed him through the door. Another thump vibrated through the floor, followed by the squeal of a cold metal window clasp and the sticky creak of the window cracking through a layer of frost as it opened. Simonsen ran towards the spare bedroom, as Danielsen turned to the bedroom on his right.

"Natsi, stop," Simonsen shouted, as he slammed into the bedroom door and caught a glimpse of a someone leaping out of the window. "Miki?"

There was a shout and scuffle on the rocks beneath the window.

"I've got a girl here," Miki said, raising his voice above the screams of a girl he had pinned to the rocks beneath his knee.

Empty bottles scattered across the floor as Simonsen ran to look, pausing at the sudden movement of a body beneath a duvet on the bed.

The bed creaked as a man fought his way free of the twists of the thin duvet, and leaped for the door. Simonsen reached for his arm, but caught a fist in his face as the man flailed out of the bedroom and into the living room, tugging at the boxer shorts sliding down his thighs.

"Danielsen," Simonsen shouted, as he pressed his hand to his nose.

He wiped a bloody palm on his vest as he staggered after the man, glancing at Danielsen as he struggled to restrain a young Greenlander on the threadbare sofa. Simonsen recognised Natsi's scowl and continued into the kitchen. He heard the crash of the front door as it slammed against the side of the house, and the tremble of feet down the wooden steps to the road.

Simonsen slipped on the ice covering the first step, gripped the banister and pulled himself to his feet. He saw the man run towards the steps leading down to the road where the police car was parked and gave chase.

The man slipped on the ice covering the road beside the communal water pump, picked himself up and ran along the road that snaked its way down the mountainside to the heliport. Simonsen climbed into the driver's seat of the police Toyota, turned on the emergency lights and reversed into the road. The man took a shortcut between the bend in the road and ran past the heliport towards the centre of Uummannaq.

Simonsen slowed to match the man's pace, drifting the police car into the middle of the road. The blue emergency lights swirled across the man's skin, and lit his breath misting in front of him. Simonsen tugged a cigarette from the packet on the dash and lit it. He wound the window down and blew out a cloud of smoke as he pulled to the right and drove alongside the young man.

"Aaju Imiina?" he asked, as he leaned his arm on the door.

"Piss off," the man said and continued running.

"Are you cold, Aaju?"

"*Aap.*"

"Then stop running and get in."

Simonsen pulled over to the side of the road and waited as the man slowed to a stiff walk and opened the passenger door. Simonsen offered him the packet of cigarettes.

"Smoke?"

The man shivered as he took a cigarette and Simonsen turned up the heat.

"Where were you going, Aaju?"

Aaju shrugged and took a long drag on the

cigarette. The smoke tumbled through his lips as he coughed. Simonsen reached between the seats and dragged his jacket through the gap, dumping it on Aaju's lap. Aaju held the cigarette between his lips as he twisted into the jacket and zipped it to the collar.

"Do you have a ticket?" Simonsen asked, as he hiked a thumb towards the heliport behind them.

"*Naamik.*"

"So you're not flying anywhere today?"

Aaju shook his head.

"Then why did you run?"

"I thought you were him."

"Who?"

"That crazy policeman," Aaju said, as he gripped the cigarette between his fingers. "You know the one? He beat up some friends in Saattut."

"Who did?"

"Some policeman."

"When?"

"Last night." Aaju shrugged.

"And that's why you ran?"

"*Aap.*"

Simonsen turned in the road and drove back to the house, parking at the bottom of the steps. He pressed the packet of cigarettes into Aaju's hand.

"Stay here," he said, and got out of the car.

The impact of his boots vibrated through the steps as he climbed them and Danielsen met him at the door. He looked beyond Simonsen at the car and smiled when he saw Aaju smoking in the passenger seat.

"How are you doing, Aqqa?"

"Come and see."

Simonsen stopped at the sink in the kitchen,

found a cloth and rinsed it. He wiped his nose as he walked into the living room, stuffing the cloth into his pocket as he nodded at Miki and then looked at the two Greenlanders sitting on the sofa with blankets around their shoulders.

"You know Natsi," Danielsen said.

"I do."

"The girl won't give her name." Danielsen grinned.

"That's alright," Simonsen said. He smiled at the girl. "Hello, Siki." She glared at him as he turned to Miki. "Sikkersoq Hermansen," he said. "Natsi's sister."

Miki slapped Danielsen on the arm. "You said you didn't recognise her?"

"I've never seen her naked before," Danielsen said and shrugged.

"That's enough," Simonsen said.

He dragged a chair to the sofa, brushed a layer of crumbs from the cushion and sat down. Sikkersoq looked away as Simonsen pulled his notebook from his pocket. The floor creaked as Miki moved to the windowsill and leaned against it.

"I have some questions," Simonsen said. "If you help me with them, then you can clean up and we'll be on our way." He waited as Natsi nodded.

"Is this about Salik?"

"Yes."

"And what about that crazy policeman?"

"About that too." Simonsen looked at Danielsen. "Go and talk to Aaju. I'll stay here with Miki."

Natsi waited until Danielsen was gone and then nudged his sister. She glared at him and pulled the blanket tighter around her shoulders.

"What can you tell me about Salik?" Simonsen said. "When did you last see him?"

"What are you going to do about the policeman?" Sikkersoq asked. "Answer that and maybe we'll tell you about Salik."

Simonsen lifted his hand as Miki stirred at the window.

"That isn't how this works," Miki said.

"No? You want our help? You help us first."

"Alright, Siki," Simonsen said. "Let's hear it."

"Some crazy guy crashed a party last night. He was mad. Fighting. They said he was a policeman. That's like police brutality or something. It's not right. Our friends were just having a party."

"Did your friends say who he was or what he wanted?" Simonsen scribbled a few details at the top of a blank page in his notebook. "What did he look like?"

"All dressed in white. Like he was hunting, they said."

"Hunting?"

"He was looking for a man."

"Where was the party? Whose house?"

"Our friend's house."

"Who owns the house?"

"That old Dane," Natsi said. "But he's never there. He's always at his cabin."

"The party was at Aksel Stein's house?"

"*Aap.*"

Simonsen sighed as he lowered the notebook. He looked at Miki.

"Maratse?" Miki whispered.

Simonsen nodded.

Chapter 12

Qitu opened his notepad and placed it on his knee. He clicked the top of his pen and watched as Tertu curled into the chair opposite him, placed the toes of her shoes on the coffee table and hid behind her knees. He had tried to offer her coffee the last time they met. Today he had cake. But Tertu, he noticed, brought her own provisions. He spotted the top of the slim can of Red Bull hidden inside her sleeve. She pulled it out, opened it and sipped as he made his notes. Tomorrow he would make sure he picked up a case of it on the way to the office.

"Palu said he put you in a hotel. Which one?" he asked. He tilted his head to see past her knee, giving him a better view of her lips.

"Nuuk Hotel."

"Is it nice?"

Tertu shrugged. "It's okay."

"Why don't we start," he said.

"Did you call your friend?"

"What?"

"The man in Uummannaq. Did you call him?"

"I sent a text. He hasn't replied."

Tertu fidgeted behind her knees and Qitu studied her hair, from the bright pink tips to the black roots. She was wearing the tusks again today. They wobbled beneath her bottom lip as she spoke and scraped the side of the can as she drank.

"I need some background, Tertu," he said. "To put things in context. Can you tell me where you grew up? What it was like at school?"

"I grew up in one of the settlements in Upernavik. My dad was a fisherman." She paused to watch as Qitu looked at her; he wrote without looking at the notepad. "How can you do that?"

"It's better if you just talk," he said. "Tell your story; pretend I'm not here."

"Okay," Tertu said and took a sip from her can. "My dad was away a lot. Mum met him in Denmark. She had problems." Tertu stuck out her thumb and little finger and pretended it was a bottle she raised to her lips. "She didn't work. Dad earned money. Some money. Most of it he drank and she drank the rest. I played outside a lot, and slept at my grandparent's house."

"What about school?"

"I didn't learn much until I moved to Upernavik for ninth grade. I lived at the students' home. I was good at Danish, which made them think I was clever. Only I really didn't know anything. I didn't go to school much, and I didn't show up for my exams."

"You moved back home?"

"*Naamik.* I met a boy and went to stay with him in Maniitsoq."

Qitu lifted his pen from the notepad and Tertu shrugged.

"Sometimes you do what people think you should do, not what your body tells you to."

"You had a relationship with him?"

"I had sex with him. He made me laugh and he had money for beer, so I stayed with him."

"Until when?"

"I met a girl. A nice one who thinks like me. I was seventeen, she was fifteen, I think."

Tertu put the can down on the floor. Her hands disappeared inside her cuffs and she folded her arms across her chest. The coffee table creaked as she trembled.

"She wasn't a lesbian. She just liked sex. She told me about these parties, where you do all kinds of things. She even said you could get money – not like being a prostitute, but because everyone was so wasted that you could take the money from their jackets and stuff."

"So you went to one of these parties?"

"I went to a lot of them. I stole lots of money, until he caught me."

"Who?"

Tertu pressed her thumbs to her mouth and stared around her sleeves at Qitu. The table creaked again and she gasped as her toes slid off the edge and her feet thudded on the floor. The coffee from Qitu's mug sloshed over the side. He mopped it up with an empty page from his notebook.

"Sorry."

"It's okay," Qitu said. He let the paper soak up the coffee and forced a smile. "You met someone at the party. He's important to the story, isn't he?"

She nodded.

"Can you tell me his name?"

Tertu shook her head.

"Maybe later then. Just tell me *about* him."

"He's smart. He knows all about the Internet. But not the regular stuff. He's into something else."

"The Dark Web?"

Tertu nodded. "He said we could make a lot of money. More than I stole at the parties."

"And you believed him?"

"He gave me money. He paid for a room in Maniitsoq. He paid for my food, and beer."

"What did you do for him?"

Tertu shifted position on the seat, tucking her heels beneath her bottom and twisting the cuffs of her sleeves in her fingers. She caught Qitu's eye.

"The first time was fun," she said. "He told me to do things with my friend."

"The fifteen year old? What was her name?"

Tertu continued as if she hadn't heard. "He made the room all dark and filmed it. Then he put it on the net. He had this website where people paid to see my video."

"A pornography site?"

"Maybe. But more than that," she said. "It was more of an *anything* site. He said that this was just the start. He gave us money and said that there was more money when we did what people asked us to do."

"Who asked you?"

"People wrote and told him what they wanted. People from all over the world. He told them how much it would be. Then we did it." Tertu slipped one of her hands out of her sleeve and turned it in the light. "He gave us one of these each time we did what they asked."

"Why?"

"Because what he did hurt me," she said, and showed him the tattoos in the joints between her fingers. "They hurt too, when he made them, but nothing like what we had to do for the camera. He said we only had to do a handful of things – two hands – and when our hands were full, we were done. We never had to do it again."

"Do what?"

Tertu shook her head. She slipped her hands out of sight and stared out of the window. Qitu checked his notes. He glanced at Tertu. He needed details, but understood that if he pushed her too quickly, he would end up with nothing. No story. No job. He had given up a lot for this. He needed to give her time. But he needed something to work on. He had to have a name or a lead, at the very least.

"Tertu," he said. "You don't want to talk about it. I understand. But can you show me the website? Maybe I can see for myself."

"You?"

"I'm a journalist, Tertu. I know how to access the Dark Web. I have the TOR browser on my Mac."

Qitu stood up at a nod from Tertu. He picked up his *MacBook* from his desk and gave it to her. Tertu's sleeves covered the keyboard, her fingers darting out of the cuffs like painted snake tongues, revealing tiny glimpses of her Aleut-tattooed fingers. She handed him the computer when she was finished.

"I have to pee," she said and walked out of the office.

The website looked like a shopping page, with padlock icons over boxes arranged in rows. Dark shapes moved with strobe-like motions, just visible behind each padlock. As Qitu moved his cursor over them a pop-up text revealed the name of the video and the amount required per minute to watch it. Bitcoin and other cryptocurrencies were the only method of payment. For ten thousand Satoshi, the smallest denomination of the Bitcoin, Qitu could see five minutes of extreme video in High Definition. Each video had the Greenlandic name of a fish, followed by the English translation. Ten thousand Satoshi, or roughly one hundred and forty US dollars, gave Qitu access to *Eqalussuaq*, the Greenland Shark. It was difficult to see, but the strobe movements of figures behind the padlock icon gave the impression of a group feeding frenzy that matched the name. He flipped through his notes and found the name Palu had used to describe Tertu. *Qaleralik*, the flat fish, halibut, a bottom feeder. For another one hundred and forty dollars he could see five minutes of what looked like bondage. But that wasn't what caught Qitu's eye. It was the box at the bottom of the page.

Qitu moved the cursor over the padlocked image on the last row of boxes and stared at the pop-up description: *Kukilik taartoq*, the black dogfish. It was the most expensive video on the page, inviting only the wealthiest of voyeurs. One Bitcoin, over six thousand US dollars, bought ten minutes of what looked like someone in captivity. The small amount of light that was in the teaser box, hidden behind the padlock, cast a shadow from what looked like a chain and cuffs of some kind, and pale brown skin. A sticker flashed beside the pop-up box with the word *live* in bold letters.

Tertu walked into the office and Qitu closed the lid of his *MacBook*. She sat down and Qitu looked at her eyes, saw the red rims as if she had rubbed them, and the wet sheen of tears.

"I'm sorry," he said.

Tertu shrugged. "It wasn't you."

"But we can stop him. You and me."

"How?"

"We go to the police."

"*Naamik*," Tertu shouted. She stood up. "No police."

"Tertu. What you had to do, what *they* have to do, we have to stop it."

"Palu said no police. Only you."

"There's a video there – it's live. Someone is chained in a black room somewhere."

"No police."

"What if he kills her? What if someone pays him to do that?"

"He'll kill me."

"You're safe, Tertu. She's not."

"I'm not safe. No-one is safe. He'll find me and kill me."

Qitu stepped around the coffee table as Tertu ran for the door. He followed her to the street, chased her along the snowy footpath towards the town centre. Thick snow caught in the headlights of cars coming towards them. One of them was a police car. Qitu barely had a moment to think before Tertu stopped and screamed. The police car slid to a sudden stop and she ran across the open ground to the right of Hotel Hans Egede, racing across the rough building ground as the police officers pressed Qitu to the side of the police car and shouted for Tertu to stop.

"Let me go," Qitu said. "It's not what you think." He twisted in the policeman's grip to see the man's lips.

"Why were you chasing her?"

"I was chasing *after* her. She's upset."

"Why?"

"We were doing an interview," Qitu said. "The questions were difficult for her."

The policeman waited as his partner gave up trying to stop Tertu and walked back to the car. He let go of Qitu and opened the passenger door of the police Toyota.

"Let's start again," the policeman said as he sat in

the passenger seat. "What's your name?"

"Qitu Kalia. I'm a journalist. Tertu was helping me with my research."

"Tertu?"

"The young woman." Qitu paused. "We were looking at something. I suggested we had to contact the police and she ran away."

"Is she a criminal?"

"No, not at all. She's a victim. And there are more. We need to find them."

"And she doesn't want to?"

"She's frightened of the consequences. She's involved in something, and she is scared for her life." Qitu wiped snow from his face and looked at the police officer.

"You believe her?"

"Yes," he said. "She needs your help."

Chapter 13

There was a small crowd of officers standing around the IT consultant's desk on the first floor of Nuuk Police station. Gaba spotted the Commissioner standing a good head taller than the officers hunched around the computer. He nodded as the Commissioner waved him over.

"What's going on?" Gaba asked.

"It's a developing situation," the Commissioner said. He pointed at the glass windows of the interview room opposite them. "Do you recognise him?"

Gaba looked and nodded. "That's Qitu Kalia."

"He's researching an article and felt the need to disclose what he had found already."

"And what's that, sir?"

"Some kind of live porn site that Kalia claims has links to Greenland. Kristian Møller, the computer guy, is confirming that now."

"Are we concerned about pornography?"

"This looks far more sinister than that. Kalia suggests it is time-critical, and he has a source who is frightened for her life. I've got people looking for her now."

"In Nuuk?"

"Yes, but this," the Commissioner said and pointed at the computer screen, "is somewhere else. See for yourself and then come find me in my office."

Gaba waited for the Commissioner to leave, and then leaned around his colleagues to look at the images on the computer. Kristian had three screens on his desk. The middle one streamed with code. The one on the left popped with messages. The third screen displayed an enlarged image of the website on the Dark Web.

"This is live?" Gaba asked.

"Yeah, it is. There's a constant stream of data, the size and speed of which indicates it is live. But the stream itself is interesting."

"In what way?"

The police officers standing around Kristian's desk moved back as he turned in his chair.

"Regular Internet users in Greenland don't have the streaming capacity for this amount of content, not without degradation of image. Plus, it's way too expensive. I think, if this is being streamed here, within the country, we're talking about a hi-tech setup using a satellite transmission, piggy-backing a cable connection in another country. It's elaborate and exclusive."

"Explain."

"It requires a high degree of technical ability, and access to expensive equipment."

"So, we're looking at someone in the telecommunications industry? TelePost?"

"Possibly, but more likely someone who studied it, not necessarily working in the industry. Not right now, anyway."

"Why not?"

"This kind of setup requires constant maintenance. Whoever is running it needs to be close to it."

"Close to the equipment or close to that?" Gaba said and pointed at the screen. He frowned as a stray thought passed through his mind at the sight of the victim's naked chest.

"Both. The camera is set up to stream."

"And what about the cost? You said this was an

expensive setup."

Kristian tapped the pop-up window on the screen.

"Bitcoin? How much is that in real money?" Gaba asked.

"It costs about two months pay to watch."

Gaba smoothed his hand over his scalp. "Alright, so he's got money. Where is he?"

"It'll take some time before we can answer that," Kristian said. He pointed at the screen with messages cascading, one window on top of the other. "I'm getting some help, but I can't tell you yet. I can say it's somewhere within North America."

"If you get closer than that, I'm your first call," Gaba said, as he took his mobile out of his pocket. "Understand?"

Gaba waited for Kristian to nod, tapping the list of contacts in his phone as he walked over to the interview room. He stared at the journalist as he waited for his call to be connected.

"Atii? You there?"

"Bad connection, but yes. I'm here."

"Get the team together, grab your gear, and meet me at the station."

Gaba ended the call, knocked once on the door and walked into the interview room. He nodded for the two police officers to leave, waited for them to close the door, and then sat down opposite Qitu.

"Now, tell me what you didn't tell them," he said.

"What?"

"Tell me what you're holding back. Anything. Doesn't matter what, just the thing you're thinking about. The answer to the question they haven't asked yet."

"I don't understand."

"Yes, you do. It's the thing you think might get you into trouble."

"I haven't done anything."

"I don't care, either way. Just tell me." Gaba slapped the table. "Don't look at them. This is me you're dealing with now, Qitu."

"I'm not a suspect."

"I don't care."

"This is an interesting technique..."

"It's the way I roll and you're wasting time," Gaba said. He stabbed his finger towards Kristian's desk. "You're wasting *her* time – the girl chained up in that dark place. In my book, that makes you an accomplice to whatever shit is going down with her. It will be on you, unless you start talking."

"I *am* talking," Qitu said. He gestured at the tape recorder between them. "I'm co-operating."

Gaba stopped the tape with a quick stab of his finger. He drummed his fingers on the table and stared at Qitu.

"Okay," Qitu said. "One thing I haven't said yet." He paused as Gaba stopped drumming the table.

"Go on."

"The teenager they found on the ice in Uummannaq. I told your colleagues that he is connected, possibly to the man or woman who runs that website. What I didn't tell them was that I contacted someone to find out more."

"Who?"

"David Maratse. I sent him a text."

Gaba cursed. "Why would you contact Maratse?"

"My source, Tertu, didn't want any police involvement. But she wanted to know if the boy's fingers were marked."

"What kind of marks?"

"Tattoos like bands on the joints of his fingers. I thought Maratse could find out."

"Because he's a private detective?"

"Because he's in the area."

"That's it?"

"Yes."

Gaba pushed back his chair and stood up. He waved for his colleagues to come in and walked to the door.

"You didn't ask *me,*" he said to Qitu. "About the boy's fingers. Of course, you couldn't know I was there." He waited for Qitu to comment, smiling at the furrow on the journalist's brow. "So, here's the answer to the question you didn't ask me. Yes," Gaba said. "The boy's fingers were banded. All the joints on the inside of his fingers."

Gaba walked across the office floor to Kristian's desk.

"You haven't called yet," he said, and waved the mobile in his hand.

"There's nothing to..."

"Work faster," Gaba said, and dialled Atii's number again.

"*Aap?*"

"Forget about coming to the station. Go to the airport. Talk to the Air Greenland desk about getting the *King Air* prepped."

"Where are we going?"

"I don't know yet," Gaba said. He jabbed his finger at Kristian. "But we'll know soon."

"It could take a while," Kristian said, his voice faltering as Gaba glared at him.

Gaba ended the call and strode across the floor to the door. It was five minutes more before the Commissioner waved him into his office. The Commissioner placed the handset of his telephone on the receiver and gestured for Gaba to sit down.

"That was the First Minister," he said.

"She knows about this?"

"No. She was passing on her condolences and wondering if we should do something for Petra. She suggested some kind of initiative or training programme in her name to commemorate Sergeant Jensen's service. I said I would think about it."

Gaba waited.

"There's something else."

"Busy day."

"Yes, but not an easy one. Have you talked to Miki?"

"Not today."

"That's impressive, if Simonsen managed to give me the message before you." The Commissioner smiled. "But that's where it stops being funny. It seems Maratse is taking matters into his own hands. Apparently, Maratse crashed a party in Saattut and beat up a couple of guys," the Commissioner said, as Gaba frowned. "Yes, I didn't believe it either."

"He's a quiet guy. It doesn't fit, sir."

"Simonsen mentioned a man called Aksel Stein. Do you remember the name?"

"Yes."

"It seems that Maratse is looking for him. Simonsen actually used the word *hunting*."

"He thinks this guy has something to do with Petra's death?"

"Possibly. And Simonsen is concerned about

what Maratse might do if he finds Stein. To be honest, given what Simonsen told me, and the reaction from the locals, I'm inclined to agree with him."

Gaba stood up and walked to the window. He tapped the glass as he stared at the icebergs in the fjord. The clouds were thinning and the sun had found a few weak spots to shine through the clouds and light the tips of the icebergs. North of Nuuk, at the top of Greenland it was dark, pitch black. Gaba thought of Maratse hunting beneath the black winter sky and wondered if it was grief that drove him, or something else? What answer would Maratse give to the question no-one was asking? Gaba felt another twist in his stomach as he thought about the video on the website, and the two months' police pay it would cost to see it. Who would he see if he could afford to watch?

"You're thinking, Gaba. I can hear you."

"What do you want me to do, sir? About Maratse?"

"He's one of our own, Gaba. We owe it to him to stop him doing something stupid. And we owe it to Petra, too. She was very fond of him."

"Yes, sir."

"This is what SRU trains for. I'm tasking you to stop Maratse before he kills someone."

"He's not a killer."

"He's armed, Gaba, and he's hunting. You need to stop him."

"What if he's right? What if it wasn't suicide?"

"Petra?"

Gaba walked to the map of Greenland mounted on the Commissioner's wall. He found Uummannaq and traced his fingers from the settlement of Inussuk to Saattut.

"It's interesting, sir, that Petra's clothes were found close to the boy's body. Simonsen suggested the two things are linked. What if Petra saw something? Maybe she tried to stop whoever killed the boy. They took her, and killed her, and then they made it look like a suicide, just to throw us off the scent."

"Coincidence."

"I don't think so. Think about Maratse. For a man who loved Petra, he was quick to bury her."

"She's gone. Maybe it helped to move on as quickly as possible?"

"With respect, sir, I know you were fond of her."

"Like a daughter, I suppose."

"But for Maratse it is so much more. I can understand where he is coming from. I talked to him at the funeral, when we walked down the mountainside. I was more upset than he was."

"He's reserved. He hides his emotions."

"It was more than that. It's like he didn't believe she was dead." Gaba rubbed his hand across his scalp. "Now that I think about it, he wasn't sad, he was impatient. Like he had something to do."

"You're making presumptions, Gaba."

"No, sir. It's starting to make sense. He arranged the funeral in a hurry because he needed to get started. Son of a bitch." Gaba laughed. "Simonsen is right. Maratse is hunting. But he's not hunting Petra's killer, he's hunting whoever took her. He thinks she's alive."

"Sergeant," the Commissioner said, as Gaba walked to the door. "I gave you a job."

"Yes, sir."

"Bring Maratse in," he said. "That's your first priority. Don't get caught up in presumptions."

Gaba nodded and dialled Atii's number as he jogged along the corridor to the stairs.

"Get on board. We're going north."

Chapter 14

The prickle of heat teased at Petra's skin, the crack, hiss and spit of wood in the pot-bellied stove worried at her ears, and the smell of smoke wrinkled her nose as she opened her eyes. Petra stared through the sticky film of tears, spit and sweat, and saw him sitting beside the stove. The funnel of his hood was dipped comically low as he read the book on his lap through a tunnel of fur. The book was lit by lantern light and the thick wick twisted black inside the oily flame. Petra could see it if she squinted, a dance of orange inside a smoky glass bulb. The wick crackled, dry like her tongue when she moved it from where it sat heavy and thick inside her mouth. The sucking noise of dry spit lifted the man's head from his book. She saw him rise, heard the chains of her cuffs scrape rusted flakes from the links as she shrank to the wall and he clumped across the dusty floorboards towards her. He tugged something black from his jacket pocket and then the orange flame was gone as he bound Petra's eyes.

"You're awake," he said.

His Danish was strong, but with an unfamiliar stress on the endings. Petra surprised herself with the analysis, wondered if she was getting stronger, or if the will to survive had taken over her senses, searching for details, filtering the dark, dust and despair for something to cling to, some kind of hope.

She heard the zip of the funnel hood, and then his voice, clearer now, as he sat down and the wooden legs of the chair creaked between the spit and crack of wood, the crackle of the flame, and the thump of her pulse.

"I've put your show on hold," he said. "You're quite the little earner. You deserve a break."

"Cold," she breathed.

"Yes, of course. No-one's watching right now."

The chair creaked, the floor vibrated, and Petra felt something heavy draped over her shoulders. A fleece-lined jacket perhaps. She turned her head, felt the chunky plastic teeth of the zip press into her cheek, and smelled the tang of old fish blood. She shivered inside the jacket, and drew her feet beneath her bottom. She could feel her rough heels on her skin, but couldn't remember if she had been wearing jeans once, when, or if, they had been removed.

"I'm sure this is strange for you, Sergeant Jensen. But we all have our part to play, you understand? I *hope* you understand. It's not so very different from what you do in your job. We both provide a service. People are needy, and you and I attend to those needs. Of course, in your work you had physical contact with the people who needed you. But let me reassure you that now, with my help, you are enhancing people's sad lives, giving them pleasure. Like I say, providing a useful service."

"You hurt me," Petra said.

"I hurt you? No," he said. "That wasn't me. *I* didn't hurt you."

Petra flinched as she realised he was close – close enough to smooth his hand through her hair. She moved her head and he let go.

"They told me what to do, and I... I had to do it, Petra. I couldn't ignore them. Why, that would be the same as you ignoring a theft, or perhaps walking over someone who had collapsed in the street. Without us to pick people up, if we don't listen to their needs, they will suffer, Petra. You do understand?"

"What you did..."

"I did it for them."

The floorboards creaked as the man kneeled in front of her. He coughed, and his breath rattled and wheezed through his lungs. Petra heard the man unscrew a bottle, and she smelled fruit and artificial sweeteners, but there was no fizz. The soft drink was flat, like she felt. The man cleared his throat. She felt him tug the tail of the jacket and pull it over her knee.

"They like watching you, Petra." He laughed. "You're a policewoman and that seems to give them a kick. I don't know why I didn't think of it before. Of course, I had to prove you were police, so I kept your ID card. Everything else is on the ice." He caught another cough in his throat and took a drink. "The note you wrote was a nice touch. It was generous of you. Now we have plenty of time. We... we can make a lot of money."

Petra moved, just a tiny bit, and felt something run from her ear. It splashed on her chest. She flinched again when the man pressed a greasy thumb onto her breast and wiped away a spot of liquid.

"Blood," he said. "It got a little rough last time. I'm sorry, of course I am, but the numbers... the numbers doubled. We had more viewers than last time."

The floor creaked as he stood up. Petra turned her head at more noises, desperate to identify them, to be sure that the twist of metal was a lid not a tool of some kind, that the bubbling of water was for coffee, and that he cursed because he dropped something, not because she screamed and bit at him – *that* she did remember – and that the soft words that followed did not disguise a sudden fleck of pain.

She smelled coffee.

She felt her body ratchet down from red alert to something more like regular fear. She recognised the sounds of spoons striking ceramic mugs, and the splash of coffee, the hiss of water on the hotplate. But then the sounds were obscured by a rush of energy and she tilted from fear to a state of terror as he freed one of her arms and stretched it to her left. The jacket slipped off her shoulders and she cried out, her breath stalling in her mouth as he fastened her wrist again.

And then he let go.

"Coffee," he said, and she heard the soft thud of the mug on the wooden floor. "Lower your hand. You should just be able to reach it."

Petra felt the rim of the mug with the tips of her fingers. There was just enough play in the chain to lift the mug to her lips, if she bent her head down, if she tilted the mug. The coffee stung her lips. The sudden rush of caffeine surged through her body and she thought about dropping the mug and ripping the blindfold from her eyes. But to what end? She was bound. Stretched. She wasn't ready for this. She wasn't prepared for someone like him.

"It's good, isn't it?" he said. "That's one of the things about this cabin, unlike the others; it's well-stocked with those little comforts that make it all worthwhile. I mean, we can work here, undisturbed. The conditions are perfect. And, with a little ingenuity, the technical challenges associated with the service can be solved."

Petra struggled with the last of the coffee as she tried to tilt the mug at the limit of the chain and the limit of her neck. The last third of the mug splashed over her lips and chin, and she lowered the mug, placed it on the floor, and wiped her chin on her shoulder.

"You want more?" he asked. "I'll make some more."

Petra listened to the now familiar noises as the man talked.

"You know this is actually rather nice. My usual co-workers are less..." he paused, tapping a spoon on the can of coffee grounds as he thought. "Well, they're not as educated. Let's leave it at that. But there is one thing they understand – it's something we agreed on, a contract of sorts. I thought about making the same contract with you. What do you think? Should we formalise this? Should we have a contract?" He waited a beat. "It's up to you, of course. But it might make it easier for you to provide the service. What do you think?"

Petra lifted her head. She heard him move, followed him with bound eyes, straining to see through the black cover tied around her head.

"Yes," he said. "Let's do this. Let's make a contract."

"What are you doing?" Petra said, as the man unhooked the chain attached to her hand. He pinched her wrist between the floor and his knee.

"It's something I learned from a friend."

Petra jerked at her hand and he pressed harder.

"Stop that, it will spoil it."

"Spoil what?"

The smell of paint or thin spirits pinched the air beneath her nose. She twisted at the sound of something being bound to what could have been a stick – hollow and dull.

"I have to use a hook," he said. "One of the thick ones they use on the boats. You know the ones I mean? I've straightened it."

"Please stop," Petra said. She gasped at a prick of metal in the skin between the joints of her little finger.

"Don't move."

She held her breath at more pricks, like tiny wet teeth biting into the first layer of her skin, and a tapping, a *tick tick tick* of fish teeth, spiny and sharp. The man splayed her fingers, his breath soft, concentrated, as he tapped the hook into the three gaps between her joints.

"You were such a star," he said, as he worked, "that I have given you three tokens on your contract."

"I don't know what you are doing. I want you to stop. Please stop."

"Shush, Petra. This is good for you. Each token I give you, each mark, is one step closer to your freedom. When your fingers are full, you are free."

She felt him wipe at her fingers, a soft cloth. And then he gripped her wrist and bent her hand towards her face. He pushed one side of her blindfold up with his thumb, angling her head in his grip so that she could only see her fingers. Petra blinked at the black bands between the joints of her little finger. Pricks of blood were creased into her skin, but the bands were solid. The man tugged the blindfold into place and fastened her wrist to the chain hooked into the wall.

"I was in Thailand," he said. "I saw some tattoos, but they were done with a machine. Then I met my friend – pretty, like you, with such pretty hands. Thin blue lines and diamonds all tapped into her skin. It gave me the idea, and I... I think it works. It's a good contract. This is iron gall ink. You can't break a contract written in ink like that."

Petra bent her finger. It pulsed beyond her view. She could still see the bands, purple-black, thick squares, and irregular rectangles. He had hurt her during the fourth change of the card, and in the first change after it; he had tagged her, made his mark. Her lower lip started to tremble and she bit it, bit it until it bled.

"You said I would be free?"

"Yes. Yes, that is the contract. And I will honour that."

"As soon as my hands are filled – all my fingers marked?"

"That's right."

Petra licked the blood from her lip, tasted copper in her mouth. She thought about being free, and then a sound from outside the cabin made her think of something else. It wasn't the sound of freedom, more like a shush and grind of ice. It reminded her of something that sounded like escape, and she pictured a man on a sledge, and bit his name into her lips, soft enough that the man would not hear, but strong enough to ignore the pain in her body, the bands on her fingers, and the fear of unfamiliar noises.

This wasn't unfamiliar.

It was hope.

Sapaat

SUNDAY

Chapter 15

Maratse saw the glow of the cabin lights and slowed the sledge with soft commands. The metal runners scraped to a stop and the rear of the sledge shimmied until it bumped against a clump of old snow, leached of moisture by the wind. Spindrift swirled across the surface as Maratse fought back a yawn. He had not slept since leaving Inussuk he'd barely rested, and he couldn't remember when he last ate a full meal, not since the funeral. He stepped off the sledge and pulled a brick of frozen *ammassat,* capelin, out of the sledge bag strung between the uprights, breaking off two or three fish for each dog. Maratse chewed on the last fish as he kneeled beside Tinka and watched the cabin.

He dug an arch in the ice as the dogs ate, looping the traces through the arch and securing the team. Maratse untied the white canvas shooting screen from the sledge and attached it to the wooden frame. He pushed the rifle through the gap in the canvas and lashed the barrel to the frame. Then he dressed, pulling the white anorak over his sealskin smock, and tugging the silk ski mask over his head. Maratse waited for the moon to slip behind the clouds, picked up the rifle and walked across the ice towards the cabin.

Hunters used the shooting screen to approach a seal on the ice. From a distance, the hunter would appear to be nothing more than an iceberg. The hunter would inch his way towards the seal, soundlessly, just as Maratse inched his way across the windblown snow beneath the cabin. The light flickered inside. Maratse watched it, searching for shadows between each increment of movement until he was at the wall, beneath the window, to the left of the door.

The wind dropped, stealing the sound from the land, stilling the snow and bursting Maratse's ears with silence. He moved to the door and opened it.

The rifle on its frame was clumsy in his grasp, and he lowered it to see the light dancing in the oil of the large soap stone lamp in the middle of the cabin. The oil was nearly spent. It must have burned for days. Maratse crossed the floor and stood beside it. He lowered the rifle and examined the cabin's only room.

The empty tins suggested it had been occupied for some time. The lamp burned but the cast iron stove was cold. There were footprints in the ashes and curved striations that could have been the tips of raven wings if Maratse hadn't seen the fish hooks and multi-coloured threads scattered beneath the stove. He bent down for a closer look, traced the marks in the ash, his fingertips a needle's breadth above the story in the soot, the marks in the ashes, the hooks beneath the fire. The shelves dipped beneath the weight of glossy literature – pornography, peeling at the edges, the models mostly male. Men with men. Men alone. Maratse put the rifle down and looked at the mattress. Soiled with grease and age, it was raised above the cabin floor on a tabletop sitting on four plastic milk crates. There was barely enough room for one sleeper, but the used condoms suggested there had been at least two.

Maratse sat down on the chair by the window. He peeled the ski mask off his head and stuffed it inside the pocket of his anorak. Once the mask was removed the scents of the cabin flooded in to his unfiltered nose. It was the smell of men, old, and young, unwashed, uncaring. A triangle of brushed wood above the door caught Maratse's eye. He studied it, standing on his toes and gripping the top of the door frame to peer at the triangular shape surrounded by old, blistered varnish. He pressed his finger into the remains of a tacky residue. Glue, fatigued by the cold. Maratse turned to look back at the bed. Whatever had been stuck on the wall above the door would have pointed right at it. There was a hole through the wall and Maratse opened the door to follow it. Four soft holes in the wood suggested something had been mounted on the outside. A sensor perhaps. But the cabin had no electricity, and it made no sense to have a sensor outside and a light within. The holes might have supported a battery box, with a lead to something inside. A camera, Maratse realised, would have a perfect view of the bed. But a battery box mounted outside the cabin would be drained by the cold. Maratse walked around the cabin, studying the walls, finding nothing.

He stopped in front of the door, lifted his foot to enter, and then paused. The snow was fresh but something had scratched at the surface to get at what lay beneath. Maratse brushed the snow to one side and revealed a patch of dark blood. He brushed more snow further from the door, until he was two metres from the cabin at the beginning of a trail. Maratse stopped brushing. He walked back to the cabin and picked up his rifle. The last of the oil burned as he left, plunging the cabin into darkness as Maratse picked up the trail and resumed the hunt.

The thump of the second hand on his watch

diminished as he allowed thoughts of Petra to recede from his mind so that he might better concentrate on the trail of blood. It twisted around the rocks, was lost – black blood on black lichen – where the snow had been blown to one side, only to reappear beneath the frantic claw marks of hungry foxes. Maratse followed the trail up towards the ridge overlooking the glacier in the next fjord.

Was it seal blood or the blood of a man, he wondered. And why did the trail lead up the mountain to the ridge? There were no reindeer here, and if there were, if the hunter had dragged a reindeer to the cabin, there would have been fur pinched between the stiff flowers of lichen, or trapped between the sharp clefts of rocks and splintered boulders. The trail led Maratse across and around all these things, but upwards, up the mountain towards the ridge.

He stopped beneath a sharp rise and slid the smooth base of the shooting screen frame – two lengths of wood-like fat sledge runners – onto the snow. He tucked the rifle butt against a rock as he pulled on the ski mask and lifted the hood of his anorak. Maratse gripped the rifle and slid it slowly over the lip as he crawled behind it. He stopped when he was flat, lying still as he scanned the ridge, a thin plateau before the steep climb down to the fjord. The blood trail was exposed, a dark swathe leading across the top of the rocks. Maratse tucked his head behind the shooting screen and slid across the wind-smoothed snow.

Hi grandfather, his *ata*, would have smiled.

"Qilingatsaq?" he would ask. "What are you doing?"

"Shush, *ata*. I am hunting."

"The screen is for the ice."

"*Iiji*, I know."

"But you are on a mountain top, Qilingatsaq. There are no seals here. There are no bears. You cannot hunt here, Qilingatsaq. Not like this."

"Shush, *ata*, you do not understand."

"It is you who does not understand." His grandfather laughed. "I will call you David."

"Why?"

"Because it is a Danish name. You are hunting like a Dane, Qilingatsaq."

"No, *ata*, I am not hunting *like* a Dane, I am hunting *for* a Dane."

"Then stand up," he said, "because Danes don't hunt like this. They don't have the patience."

Maratse frowned as the voice of his grandfather brushed against the snow beneath his rifle. He let out a soft laugh as he pushed himself onto his knees, and then stood up. Petra didn't have time for him to be patient. Maratse cradled the rifle in his arms and jogged across the ridge to the other side. At the bottom of the mountainside, perhaps three hundred metres below Maratse, the sea ice fused with the land. Maratse followed the direction of the blood trail and saw a dark shape on the ice, with another one hundred metres from the land. He unlashed the rifle and left the screen and frame on a large black rock. He picked his way down the mountain, slipping the soft soles of his sealskin *kamikker* across the exposed rocks and through the pockets and pillows of snow, all the way to the ice foot.

He lifted the rifle to his shoulder and centred the sights on the middle of the dark shape. It was too far to see. He climbed over the ice foot and walked along the ice, shushing the soles of his feet across the surface with reckless impatience.

The blood from the cabin led here. There were answers here. Maratse was meant to come here. He knew this, and the body of the man splayed on the ice behind the snow scooter confirmed it.

Maratse stared at the entrance hole of the rifle bullet in the middle of Aksel Stein's forehead. But the bullet had not killed the man. Maratse leaned over him, saw the ragged knife wound in Aksel's stomach, and looked back up the mountainside towards the ridge, beneath which was the cabin. Aksel was naked, his clothes strewn across the ice, frozen in acts of escape, as the wind teased at the flaps before the snow hardened and secured the corners. It reminded Maratse of the scene at Petra's suicide spot and he wondered for a moment if that was significant. Was there something he should be considering, beyond the hunt for the Dane, now that the hunt was over? Was there a message hidden here? What was it? Who left it? Who was it for?

Maratse ignored the clothes and examined the snow scooter. He slung the rifle over his shoulder and opened the compartment beneath the seat. Maratse found a camera attached to a triangular mount beside a box with four screws, one in each corner. The camera battery was dead, and the box contained a battery pack that looked like it could be attached to a more robust supply of power, like a generator. There was an SD card inside the camera. Maratse thought about taking it, but he would need a computer, to see it, and the nearest computer was one night away by sledge.

His watch reminded him of moments passing, as the thump of the second hand grew stronger.

Petra was running out of time.

Maratse put the camera inside the seat compartment and closed it, securing the clasps to seal it from the snow. This was evidence, someone was meant to find it, he just wasn't sure it was meant to be him.

He was hungry, cold and tired. Maratse warmed up on the climb back up the mountainside. He picked up the shooting screen, carried it across the ridge and past the cabin. The interior was dark, the soap stone lamp extinguished, and the stars pricked at the night sky. Tinka was the first dog to react as Maratse crossed the ice to the team. He greeted her with a soft pinch of her ears before he walked to the sledge, pulled a chocolate bar from the sledge bag, and dug into his gear to find his mobile phone. He slipped a cold hand inside his sealskin smock and teased the slim battery for the mobile from a pocket Buuti had sewn inside the smock. He powered up the phone and cast a hopeful glance at the stars, that this area of Uummannaq might be blessed with good service. Two bars out of four were better than he had hoped. Maratse fumbled through the short list of contacts Petra had keyed into his phone and selected one of them.

"Karl," he said once the dial tone ended and a short brush of static crackled on the line. "I need your help."

Chapter 16

A stream of families and youth groups shushed past the cultural centre. Qitu watched them, stunned for the moment that he could hear the legs of their salopettes rubbing, the soft thuds of mittens on duvet jackets, and the occasional shriek of laughter as a father chased his young son, or a sister chased her brother. Children were having fun, on their way to the shopping centre to see Father Christmas. Qitu plucked his hearing aids out of his ears and pocketed them. He walked down the steps from the police station and turned right out of the parking area, following the broad, snowy road to the sea.

He sat on the bench beside the *qajaq*s. The statue of Sedna was coated in snow, and the little wall at the base of the statue did little to deter the tiny growlers of ice bumping at the sculpted mammals and fish swirling around her naked body, twisting into her hair, teasing her. Qitu pressed his hand to his mouth and stared through Sedna to a much darker place where another naked woman was twisted into positions he tried not to imagine. Gaba Alatak called him an accomplice, and even the most rational part of Qitu's mind couldn't convince Qitu otherwise. He *felt* responsible, as irrational as that may be.

Qitu pressed the tips of his shoes into the snow beneath the bench. He stared at Sedna, tried to plug into the mother of the sea as if she might have the answer. *Any* answer. He felt responsible for two women, and no matter what he might achieve with the publication of his article, he couldn't write fast enough. This would be an *expose* of the underground Greenland sex industry with international links. In reality, he had yet to write a single word. He knew that words alone wouldn't save Tertu, or the woman in the video. He needed facts, something to work with, to analyse and dissect for details, perhaps even a location. He could waste time looking for Tertu, or he could wait for her to come to him. In the meantime, he could make an effort to locate the woman in the video. He tasted bile at the thought, swallowed and stood up. Qitu took one last look at Sedna, and walked back towards the town centre.

He caught the bus to his apartment, packed a bag and picked up the charger for his phone. He emptied the cupboard of coffee, bread and noodles, took cheese and reindeer meat from the fridge. If Tertu was going to find him, he had to be in the office, for as long as it took the police to find the woman. He locked the door and caught the next bus on its loop back into town.

It was snowing, harder now than before. The road outside the NMG office was dark and empty, with only a handful of people visible through the window of the CrossFit gym. Qitu kicked the snow from his boots and opened the door.

He sent a text to Palu as he cooked the reindeer meat, slicing it into thin steaks and pressing it into the slices of white bread. He felt the incoming text vibrate through the counter and checked Palu's response. Qitu's mouth stretched forgotten muscles into a smile – his first since he had met Tertu in the café. Palu's text suggested that the Berndt Media Group had a very guilty conscience because of what happened in Berlin. His request for funds had been approved with the proviso that Qitu could link his expenditure to the investigation. He texted that he could, but wondered how he would document his spending, and if that documentation might put him behind bars.

There's no other way, he thought, as he carried his sandwich into the office and typed the password into his computer. He wondered for a second if he should have eaten, if it wasn't better to work on an empty stomach. Qitu pushed the sandwich to one side. Once he had created an account, bought two Bitcoins, and opened the TOR browser, he forgot all about being hungry.

The website contained a string of code that identified Qitu's screen capture software. A pop-up window over a blank screen advised him to turn it off before he continued. Qitu grabbed his mobile, plugged in the charger, and held it front of the screen. The image of the website flickered until the camera in his mobile compensated. Qitu taped his mobile to the arm of the desk lamp, clicked on the padlock covering the black dogfish video and entered the details required to transfer the payment. He paused before the final click, pressed his hand to his mouth and took a moment. He reasoned that it was necessary, that he had to do this. He was an investigative journalist, this was his assignment. The thought that exposure to such material might affect him crossed his mind. He snorted at such concern, reminding himself that he was in no danger, that it was the woman in the video who was suffering. Watching her didn't make him an accomplice. He would be abandoning her if he didn't. And it was not as if the police would be paying to view the content. They didn't have the budget.

Qitu confirmed the transaction with a click.

The padlock icon faded and the video window

drifted to the edges of Qitu's screen. Living in a world with limited sound required an extra step to remember that it was available. Qitu reached for the hearing aids in his pocket and stopped. He swallowed, his tongue dry, as the camera zoomed in on the face of a woman, her long black hair taped to the sides of her head to reveal her face, as a gloved hand smeared thick lipstick across her lips and onto her cheeks. A cursor flashed in a live chat box beneath the image. Qitu read what was going to happen next. He grabbed the waste paper basket beneath the desk as the bile turned to vomit and he emptied his stomach.

Qitu clutched the basket to his chest and walked around the office, glancing at the top right corner of the screen to see how many minutes remained before the padlock returned and he was kicked off the session. He had two minutes. Another glance at the main image drew him closer to the screen as the camera shifted to focus on the woman's fingers. Her little finger was banded with three tattoos, just like Tertu's. The camera image wobbled as if the operator was pulling it closer. Qitu saw what looked like an industrial fish hook, bent straight, harpoon-like. He watched as it was dipped into a dark liquid and then something obscured the camera again as the man shifted his hands and Qitu saw a flash of white as someone tapped the hook into the joints between the woman's fingers. The image paused as the padlock faded into focus. The woman had three more bands on her fingers.

It was over, Qitu realised. At least it was for him. He clicked out of the TOR browser and checked his mobile. Qitu started the transfer of the video to his *MacBook* and then made coffee in the kitchen. Strong coffee. He pushed his hearing aids into his ears, waited for the coffee machine to finish spitting and spluttering, and then took the whole can and a mug into the office. Qitu drank two mugs of coffee while he waited.

He removed his hearing aids after the first minute of video. He closed the lid of his *MacBook*, took a breath and pulled out his notebook. He would start with the text, transcribing it onto paper before typing it up. Focusing on the text removed the intimacy. It read like a poorly-scripted porn movie, full of bad spellings, bad grammar and bad intentions. Qitu almost laughed at the child-like English language. Almost. He focused on the sound next, adjusting his hearing aids and tilting his head to one side to capture as much detail as possible. He filled his notepad with an audio description that turned the porn movie into a chilling horror film.

Qitu took a break, emptied his bladder, emptied the waste paper basket, made more coffee, cleaned the sink and started on the mould in the fridge.

"Stop," he said. "Just get it done."

He filled his coffee mug, wondered if he could muster a casual approach to watching the video – a professional objectivism, and then realised he couldn't. Qitu sat down and played the video for the third time, pulling his eyes away from the live chat to actually look at what was happening on screen.

Behind the lipstick, beneath the tears on her cheeks, the tic of muscles around her eyes, Qitu saw a face he recognised. He reached for his mobile, dropped it and bent down to pick it up. When he looked up he saw Sergeant Petra Jensen, her face pressed to the camera, and a dull distant look in her eyes.

This can't go on, he thought. *It has to stop.*

Qitu opened the thread of texts he had sent to Maratse and wrote one more. The urgency of each message increased from the first to the last. But it was hopeless, of course, even if Maratse looked at his mobile, even if he read his messages, where would he go? How would he find her? He read the last message one more time and pressed *send*.

PETRA IS ALIVE.

For the moment, at least. She had six bands on her fingers. Qitu looked at his hands. The thumbs had space for two bands each, and three on each finger. Petra had six bands already. If he filled a finger after each... Qitu struggled to find an adequate description. He settled on *session*. Petra had eight sessions left, before her hands were full and she was free.

But what kind of freedom? According to Gaba, the fingers of the dead teenager were fully banded. Loyalty was slavery and freedom was death. Petra was going to die.

Qitu closed the lid of his *MacBook* and stuffed it into his satchel. He pressed his notes into the sleeve in the back, and tucked his mobile into his pocket. He scribbled a note for Tertu and taped it to the office door on his way out.

He took the pedestrian street between the shops on his way to the police station, bumping shoulders with parents and dodging children. They carried paper bags full of sweets from Father Christmas, swapping treats and pressing toffees into their mouths as they walked. Qitu tucked his arm around his satchel and jostled his way to the side of the street. With his head down he didn't see Greenland's First Minister as she touched him on the arm. He recoiled into the wall of the supermarket and stumbled. Nivi Winther steadied him with her hand and he turned to look at her face.

"I'm sorry, Qitu. I startled you."

Qitu leaned against the wall and took a breath.

"Are you alright?"

"I'm alright," he said. "But..."

"What's wrong, Qitu? You look pale. Are you sick?"

"It's Petra."

"Petra Jensen? Yes, I know. I'm so sorry, Qitu. Did you know her well?"

"No, I mean..." Qitu stuttered.

How much did she know? he wondered. Did she have some kind of briefing from the Police Commissioner, or did she just read the police reports the following day? Qitu smoothed his jacket and repositioned his satchel, thinking of the consequences of bringing the First Minister into a police investigation. The image of Petra, lipstick smeared across her face, her fingers banded and bruised, the horror soundtrack and the immature grammar of torture and pain set his jaw and he made a decision.

"I am on my way to the police station," he said. "Petra is alive."

Chapter 17

They flew through the night. The SRU team was quiet. Peter tried to sleep. Atii cast furtive glances at Gaba as the team leader mulled over his responsibilities and tried to identify the parameters within which the mission success might be measured. Maratse had to be stopped, for his own protection. The Commissioner had been vague about how, but you don't send the SRU to talk softly. You send Gaba and his team to act – hard and fast, to respond to any given situation in which violence is likely. The SRU was trained to be flexible, disciplined, but effective. Maratse had been identified as a threat, a fact that no doubt pleased Simonsen who would feel vindicated at last. Uummannaq's Chief of Police was also in charge of the investigation, although Gaba retained operational command. But how would Maratse react?

He remembered working with Maratse in Nuuk a long time ago, years before the Tinka Winther case. Maratse was investigating a missing persons case, and Gaba just happened to have stumbled upon a person of interest in a drug bust. Petra was there too. She was just a Constable back then. She was the one to talk Maratse down when the suspect played hard to get. Maratse had a temper, or, rather, he had the potential for violence, if you pushed the right buttons. If Maratse had an idea who might have abducted Petra – if she had been abducted – then it was safe to assume that Maratse's buttons had been well and truly pressed.

If he was right, Gaba thought. *What then?* What was the appropriate SRU response? What was his own? Hadn't Gaba insinuated that he and Maratse could help each other, just as soon as Miki discovered a lead? Clearly, Maratse had leads of his own, and his own method of finding more. That was what was getting him into trouble and forcing Gaba and Maratse on a collision course.

Atii tapped his knee.

"Are you alright?"

"I'm fine, just thinking," he said.

"I met him you know."

"Maratse?"

"Yep, at the airport in Nuuk. Petra was meeting him there. She'd just broken up with you." Atii paused. "We weren't all that close, but I miss her, you know?"

Gaba nodded.

"Anyway, Maratse got off the plane. He was with Nivi Winther. I think she hired him."

"She did."

"Is he like a private investigator or something?"

"I think people want him to be," Gaba said. "But he doesn't solve things as such; they just seem to evolve around him. I think that's what bugs Simonsen so much."

"And now? Who's he working for?"

"No-one. And that's what makes him dangerous."

"So, we're going to stop him?"

"*Aap*," Gaba said. The decision was made. He would operate within the law, to the very letter of the law, and stop Maratse before he did something stupid. He owed Petra that at the very least.

"We're landing," Atii said. She turned in her seat, tightened the belt around her lap and took Gaba's hand.

"Constable?"

"Flying is alright," she said. "But I don't like landing. There's too many things that can go wrong. Like wind shear," she said, as the small twin-turboprop engines surged in the wake of a sudden gust, the tail end of a catabatic wind from the mountains above the gravel landing strip in Qaarsut.

She held Gaba's hand until they landed, and the pilot taxied the *King Air* to the airport building. Danielsen met them at the plane and helped them carry the gear to the back of the police car. He yawned as he climbed in behind the steering wheel.

"We're on a budget," he said. "So, I'm driving to Uummannaq. Don't fasten your seatbelts," he said and grinned. "There's a few leads opening up in the ice."

Gaba glanced at Atii.

"What?" she said.

"Leads in the ice? That's open water, Atii."

"So? We're in a car." She slapped Peter on the shoulder and dipped her head towards Gaba. "He thinks I'm scared."

Peter said nothing, but Gaba saw him fiddle with the seatbelt. *We need to* focus, he thought. The sooner they were briefed the better.

"Is Simonsen in the office?"

"He said I should take you to the hotel. He'll brief you first thing tomorrow."

"And Miki?"

"Waiting at the hotel."

Danielsen sped across the ice, slowing only at the spot where the leads had formed a ridge in the road as the plates of sea ice fused, cracked and froze in pressure ridges with the changing of the tides. He bumped the police car over the ridge and accelerated towards Uummannaq. Ten minutes later he parked outside the hotel. Miki helped them unload, and gave them the keys to their rooms.

"Get some rest," Gaba said, with a nod towards the stairs. He waved as Danielsen got into the car and then steered Miki into the dining room. "Catch me up," he said, and poured a cup of coffee.

"We still can't connect the two investigations," Miki said, as he sat down at a table by the window. The street lights turned the snow into the colour of brushed peaches. Teenagers walked in groups beneath the lights. They would be late for school the next morning, or they would sleep in class. Miki watched them pass.

"Miki?"

"Sorry," he said. "We picked up three people yesterday. A brother and sister from Uummannaq and a guy from Nuuk."

"Name?"

"Aaju Imiina. I don't know him. He's sleeping in one of the cells. The sister kicked him out of her bed."

"I'll talk to him tomorrow," Gaba said.

"Simonsen won't like that."

"Then you'll distract him."

"Sure." Miki nodded.

"What about Maratse?" Gaba almost said *Petra*, but he caught her name on his tongue before it slipped out.

"Sikkersoq, the sister, said something about a policeman beating up people at a party. Danielsen confirmed it with a phone call and was given a description that matched Maratse. We have the location of a cabin that Aksel Stein is known to use, and Simonsen has chartered a helicopter for first thing tomorrow morning. No expense spared."

"Good," Gaba said. "What do we know about Stein?"

"He has a history of abuse – alcohol and physical. His kids were taken away from him, twice, from two different partners. The oldest of the kids was the one Danielsen talked to. He's living in Aksel's house. He hasn't seen his dad in over a week. It's not unusual, apparently. And he didn't think to go looking for him. He doesn't want to see him when he's drunk."

"Anything else? Other vices we should know about?"

"There was some mention about boys, or young men, but nothing confirmed. We'd have to pick him up to find out. So..."

"Tomorrow. Sure."

Gaba walked across the room and returned with the coffee pot.

"What do you think about Maratse?" he asked, as he sat down.

"Do I think he's after Stein? Yes. Definitely."

"Should we let him?"

"Sir?"

"If Maratse is looking for Petra's killer, maybe we should just give him a chance. Turn a blind eye for a moment. What do you think?"

Miki twisted in his seat. He looked at the door for a second, and then back at Gaba.

"Is this a test?"

"Maybe." Gaba topped up his coffee.

"I don't know," Miki said. He glanced over his shoulder at the bar. "If you were asking me over a beer..."

"So, get a beer."

Miki drummed his fingers on the table. He looked at the bar and laughed.

"I don't need a beer," he said. "I would stop him, *before* he did something stupid. Petra wouldn't want him to do anything like that. We owe her."

"And if she's alive and he's onto something. Would you stop him then?"

"This is all hypothetical, right? I mean, Petra committed suicide."

"You really believe that? That Sergeant Jensen would crawl through the ice?"

Miki shook his head. "No."

"Neither do I. But I'm struggling with this, Miki. I need you to be the check and balance to my decisions these next few days. If we're in that position, and we can see – clearly, mind you – that Maratse knows something or has a lead that might lead to Petra, I need to know that if I look at you..."

"We stop him if we have to, Gaba. We do what's right."

Gaba made a fist and rapped his knuckles softly on the table. "Okay," he said. "Now get some sleep."

"Yes, boss," Miki said. He paused at the bar on his way to the door. "Did I pass the test?"

"Sure," Gaba said.

Miki nodded and walked to the door, it creaked as he opened it. Gaba listened to him thump up the stairs. He finished his coffee and refilled the cup. He felt his mobile vibrate inside his pocket. He pulled it out and clicked on a new message. Kristian Møller was working late it seemed. Gaba called him.

"Yes?"

"Gaba?" Kristian said. "There's been a development. The journalist paid to access the video. He has made a positive identification of Sergeant Jensen."

"What?"

"The woman in the video. It's Petra Jensen. The First Minister has confirmed it too."

"Nivi Winther?"

"It's a long story. Apparently they bumped into one another and..."

"Kristian."

"Yeah, sorry. We've got ten minutes of video. Qitu recorded it on his phone. We're processing the audio for any clues as to location."

"What about the video?"

"It could be anywhere. It's too dark. The audio is our best bet. But the quality isn't great." Kristian paused. "He transcribed the chat messages. I can send them to you in a mail. The audio and video is too big to send with standard connection rates. You won't have broadband in Uummannaq."

"Send it to my mobile," Gaba said.

Petra is alive.

"You're sure? That's going to be expensive."

"Kristian, let's be clear about this, if you're not uploading it the second we're done talking..."

"I understand."

"What about the Commissioner?"

"He's on his way in."

Gaba thought about the *King Air*. The pilots said they were close to their maximum flying time. They would rest at Qaarsut. Gaba needed to keep them there if Kristian discovered the location and they needed to fly. He almost laughed. Of course they would need to fly. He had to keep the plane on the ground, just in case.

"Listen, you need to get the Commissioner to give us the plane. We have to have priority. No medical emergency take precedence. Not right now."

"I'm not sure..."

"Just give the Commissioner the message. He can work it out."

"Right."

"One last thing – you don't leave your desk."

Gaba ended the call and pushed his chair back. He grabbed his travel bag from the corridor and pounded up the stairs.

"Miki?" Gaba shouted, as he paused between the two wings of the hotel.

"What's up?"

"We're meeting in the dining room in five minutes. Get everyone downstairs."

Gaba brushed past Miki and opened the door to his room. He flung his bag on the bed and pulled the phone charger from the inside pocket. He stopped to take a breath. With little or no rest on the plane, the team was tired. But they needed to stay on top of this. He would brief them while the video uploaded to his mobile. A message from Kristian confirmed it was uploading, but the two bars of service on his phone suggested it was going to take some time. Time they could use to plan. Maratse just dodged a bullet, maybe even literally, as his status was de-prioritised. But then, if he was already on the trail of the man responsible for taking Petra, Gaba might have to split the team to find him. He searched for Simonsen's number in his list of contacts. It was time to wake up the Chief.

Chapter 18

Something was ticking. Petra could hear it, but it was far away. She tried to turn her head but a dull ache in the base of her skull stopped her. She tried to swallow, drawing her tongue to the centre of her mouth. It stopped in the middle, like a truck jamming the highway, wheels dry with raw rims, the tread of the tyres almost gone, the metal poking through the rubber, dull slivers of steel. The ticking continued, and then paused, only to start again. She could feel it now. A pricking on her fingers. Petra opened her eyes. Her eyelashes, thick and heavy, scratched against the blindfold. It was bright, and the light in the cabin pressed through the black cloth. She moved her eyes; saw the shape of something, *someone*, hunched over her arm. She could feel a weight pressing on her wrist and she knew it was him, that she was being marked, and she closed her eyes. Petra sighed at the thought of freedom, her soft breath, barely audible, pushed past her broken down tongue. He was marking her, counting down her freedom. If only she could see her hand, she would know she would soon be free, that he would let her go. He was the only one who could set her free. *No-one else.* Not even Maratse. She felt a twinge of something – anger perhaps. It tremored through her body and it turned the man's head.

He must be finished, she thought, as the ticking stopped and she heard the air rattle in his lungs as he took a breath before speaking.

"Petra," he said. "You're awake. Let me help you."

She felt his hands on her bare arms, a brush of something wet on her skin before he thumbed it away. It might have been ink. *Freedom*, she thought, as he helped her sit up.

"You're weak," he said. "I'm not surprised. That was a tough session. You are probably sore, all over. Let me find something to warm you up."

Petra listened to him clump across the floorboards. She drew her left hand to her body. It was free. She pulled it all the way to her lap. Then she tested the chain on her right hand. Petra almost laughed as she felt the rough scratch of the floorboards on her knuckles. There was no chain. She rested her palms in her lap, pressed the tips of her fingers into a light touch. Euphoric. That's how she felt. To feel one's own touch after so long. She would have smiled, if her bruised lips didn't hurt quite so much. She looked up at the sound of the man returning, and smiled at his shadow as he draped a thick blanket around her shoulders.

"Thank you," she whispered, her voice hoarse – that damn truck, parked in the way of everything.

"Do you want to see your hands?"

Petra's breath caught in her throat.

"Yes."

She understood that there were things after the pain, there was something after that. Her hands were free, and then it went dark as he leaned around her, his arms on each side of her head, rough fingers tugging at a thick knot of cotton that caught in her hair and pressed into her skull. Perhaps it was that causing her head to ache? Petra didn't know, but a second later she didn't care, as the knot loosened and the blindfold slipped over her face, tickled her nose and hung around her neck. She realised his face was not hidden and she dipped her head quickly, averting her eyes.

"You can look at me, Petra," he said. "You've earned that."

"Not yet," she whispered.

"Of course." He took a step backwards. "Your hands."

Petra started to shake; her breath lumped in her throat, pressing past her tongue from both sides, in and out, short breaths as she looked down at her fingers, saw the fresh pricks of blood and ink tracing the thin lines on her skin. She flattened her hands against her thighs, palms up. She gasped when she saw the bands on her fingers. All of them.

"Your thumbs," he said. "They are always tricky, so I left them 'til last."

"Last?"

"Yes, Petra. One last session, and you're free."

Petra felt a shiver grip her shoulders. It rippled down her arms and made her hands shake. She curved her back and lowered her head, felt her hair tickle her skin as it slipped from her shoulders. She tried to draw her knees up to her chest, but found that she ached in other places too, like her hips, as if they had been pressed. Her legs were sore. Her whole body was sore. It crumpled her, but he was there to help her. Somehow he helped her to her feet and they moved slowly, so slowly across the floor to a bed.

"I'm sorry," she said. "I'm so slow."

"It's okay," he said. "Let me help you."

The sheets on the bed were soft and warm, as if someone had just crawled out of it. She let him help her onto the bed, felt the blanket slip from her shoulders, and then he pulled the sheets over her body, tucking the edges around her neck. Petra slipped her hands up through the sheets and stared at her fingers as he draped the blanket on top of her.

"Tattoos are powerful things," he said, as he walked away from the bed and sorted things in the small kitchen area. "Symbolic. I only wish I was better at doing them. You deserve better. Of course, I'll get better over time."

Petra stared at her thumbs.

One more session. The last one.

"I was telling you about my friend. Do you remember? The one with the tattoos on her fingers. She had them done in Alaska and then more here at home." He filled a pan with water, splashed oil into a saucepan. He coughed for a moment and then continued. "She never said exactly what they meant, or what significance they had. That's part of the magic," he said, as he cracked two eggs into the pan. "You must be hungry. I have bacon too."

Petra heard him twist the cap off a carton of orange juice. He carried it over to her, stepping around the camera. She noticed the red light was on as he held the glass to her lips. She winced as the tart juice stung her lips, but it loosened her tongue.

"Better?"

"Yes," she said.

She looked into his eyes, a deep brown like her own. He had a strong jaw peppered with a light stubble, black like his thick brows and the neatly cut hair on his head. He smiled. Petra looked away as something started spitting on the hotplate.

"Eggs," he said. He placed the glass on the floor and thumped across the floorboards to save the eggs. The water started boiling and he slipped two more eggs into the pan. "I like to dip bread into mine," he said.

Petra saw him flick his head towards the window. The glass was hidden behind heavy curtains. She watched as he walked to the window, lifted one corner and peered out. The sky was dark but not black. Petra felt the midday twilight tug at her eyes, and she stared past him. She continued staring as he let the curtain fall and walked back to the kitchen area.

"I'm sure you'd like some fresh air," he said, as he lifted the pan to slide the eggs onto a plate. "But it's too dangerous right now."

"Dangerous?" Petra felt her skin tighten as she frowned.

"Yes. I need to do something before we can go outside."

"Will I be able to go out?" she asked. "When I am free?"

"Of course. Everything will be sorted by then." He turned and smiled at her. "Are you hungry?"

Petra apologised when she spilled the food on her chin. The fork shook in one hand and the plate wobbled in the other. It all felt so unfamiliar, as if she hadn't eaten before, or as though her body had forgotten how to move the fork from the plate to her mouth. He helped her again. She felt his light touch as he took the plate from her hand, cut the bacon and egg and bread into pieces, and lifted small forkfuls into her mouth.

"Thank you," she said, as she licked yolk from her swollen lips.

Her tongue, at least, was behaving. He smiled as he pressed the fork into the last mouthful. She saw him glance to one side, and followed his gaze to the camera. She felt her stomach cramp. Felt the food rise up to her mouth.

"Don't mind them," the man said. "They can wait. You need food. You need to sleep. And soon you will be free." The fork scratched across the plate as he chased an errant piece of bacon fat. "Open wide," he said. "Last piece."

He started coughing as she chewed, and suddenly the camera was forgotten. He was ill. She could see that. The bed shook as the cough took hold of him and he struggled for breath. Petra watched, eyes wide. He needed help. She could almost feel the joints of her fingers weep as the ink settled and mixed with the blood beneath her skin. Petra glanced at the camera, her body tense, and then the man stopped coughing, pressed his hand on the bed to steady his body, and she felt the press of his fingers on her leg.

"I'm alright," he said and smiled.

"What's wrong with you?"

"I have a cold. It might be the flu. I've been coughing for weeks. I sweat at night too," he said and twisted a corner of the bed sheet in his hand. "You can probably feel that. I'm sorry."

Petra knew what he had. A part of her brain clicked out of her body, removed itself from the cabin, the pain, the red light of the camera, and the bands of ink tapped into her fingers. He had tuberculosis. She was sure of it. He was sick, just like so many people in Greenland, especially in the settlements.

"You need help," she said.

"I'll be alright."

"No." Petra tried to straighten her back, but the pain in her stomach and her hips stopped her. *Why do*

I have to be so weak, she thought.

"It's you we have to worry about," he said. "Sleep now. Get your strength back."

"What about you?"

"I'll be fine," he said. He wiped his hand across his mouth and frowned at the spot of blood on his skin. "Get some rest."

Petra lay back on the pillow and watched as he put the plates on the counter and crossed to the window. He lifted the curtain once more and she heard him curse. There was a soft crack, like wood tearing, and a dull thud that could have been something heavy pounding or flattening something. Petra had a strange thought of the neighbours throwing things into a skip, tidying up the house. The image blurred as she closed her eyes, ignored the pain in her stomach, and turned her head to one side, brushing her nose beneath the white sheets. White like the snow quilting the ice, and a figure somewhere in the distance, out of reach, fading. She heard the neighbours break another piece of wood and then let the mattress tug her body into sleep as she searched one last time for the figure in white.

What was his name?

Ataasinngorneq

MONDAY

Chapter 19

The hotel dining room buzzed with activity. Simonsen moved to one side as Danielsen bumped past him carrying a large flat-screen television. He watched the young Constable position the television on a table at one end of the room, pulling leads and power cables out of a shopping bag, as he hooked the screen up to a computer. Simonsen thought he recognised it.

"Is that my computer, Aqqa?"

"*Aap.* I took it from your desk."

"Why?"

"Because it's faster than mine."

"And the flat-screen? That looks like yours."

Aqqa grinned. "Don't tell my girlfriend?"

"What girlfriend?"

Danielsen winked and pulled another handful of cables out of the plastic bag. Simonsen wasn't finished. He took a step towards him and stopped when Gaba called his name.

"You're late," he said.

"I had to let Aaju out of his cell."

"You let him go?"

"We had nothing on him." Simonsen waved his hand at the activity in the dining room. "What's all this?"

"This is the situation room," Gaba said. "Your police station is too small."

"And this is too public and expensive," Simonsen said, as the hotel owner held the door of the kitchen open for a member of staff carrying a tray of refreshments to the table. "I don't have the budget for this."

"Relax. Nuuk is paying."

"Because of a video?"

"Because Petra is in the video, Chief." Gaba pointed at Danielsen. "Once we've got the screen up we'll run it through there. There's about seven minutes before it downloads."

"And Maratse?"

"Was right. Petra's not dead."

"If he was so sure, then why the hell did he arrange a funeral?"

Gaba sighed. "I would have done the same," he said. "Just to get you and everyone else off my back."

"It was a distraction. He knows more than he's saying. He might even be involved somehow."

"You don't believe that, Chief."

"No," Simonsen said. "But we need results. This," he said and gestured at the SRU officers helping Danielsen hook up the computer, "is all very elaborate. You'll have the whole town looking through the windows."

"Listen, Chief. I don't care about how this looks. Petra is out there somewhere, alive and in trouble. The only *result* I'm interested in right now is her safe recovery. If that means we let Maratse run rampage through the settlements. Fine. So be it. If it means he busts a few heads in the process. I can live with that. But I won't let you slow this down because of how it looks. I have tactical command for situations like this. Are we clear?"

Simonsen glanced at Miki as he hovered by Gaba's side. He saw the start-up screen of his computer blink onto Aqqa's flat-screen television, just as the kitchen staff set up the breakfast buffet. He patted the pockets of his jacket and found his cigarettes, sticking one between his lips as he tapped his lighter against his thigh.

"Just remember, I've chartered a helicopter. Whatever happens here, I'm sending Aqqa to Aksel's cabin and I want your team with him. It's the one lead we've got, and whatever else you discover in this situation room of yours, is secondary to the cabin."

"Unless new evidence..."

"If you can confirm a location from the video, the chopper's yours, Sergeant. We're clear on that."

"Thank you," Gaba said. He nodded at Miki.

"The video has downloaded. We're ready to see it."

"And you can run it through the Chief's computer?"

"It's on your Micro SD card and Aqqa has an adapter. We're good to go, boss."

"Alright." Gaba took a breath. "Let's do it."

Simonsen caught the kitchen staff loitering by the buffet bar and waved them into the kitchen. He locked the door to the dining room and cursed the lack of curtains.

"We're ready," Aqqa said and he gestured for Simonsen to join them.

The six police officers stood in a semicircle around the flat-screen, obscuring the image from anyone looking through the windows from the street below, and blocking the view from the kitchen if a curious member of staff looked through the tiny square of glass set in the door.

"There's no sound," Danielsen said. "I forgot the speakers."

"That's alright, Constable," Gaba said. "Just play it as soon as you're ready."

As the image clicked onto the screen, the only sound in the dining room was the whir of the computer fan and a series of low gasps between them as the image of Petra flickered into focus.

"Motherfucker," Gaba whispered.

Simonsen felt the cigarette fall from his lips as the camera captured images of Sergeant Petra Jensen and the shadow of a man twisting and pulling her in different directions with different implements like a deranged puppeteer, cavorting to some demonic dirge that only he could hear.

"Chief," Danielsen said, and then again, louder. "Chief."

"What?" Simonsen pulled away from the screen and looked at the young Constable.

"Your phone."

Simonsen heard it then, and pulled the phone from his pocket. He caught Gaba's eye and then walked away from the screen. Simonsen unlocked the dining room door and took the call outside.

"Simonsen," he said, as he took in a breath of cold air outside the hotel entrance.

"You need to come."

"Who is this?"

"You need to come to the dock, now, Chief."

The caller hung up and Simonsen jogged to the car. He glanced at the hotel as he backed onto the road. He wasn't sure he could cope with much more of the video, and Gaba knew how to reach him. Simonsen looked at his watch, saw that there was a little less than an hour before they had to be at the heliport, and then drove to the docks.

A man wearing the plastic overalls they used in the fish factory waved as Simonsen drove onto the dockside. Simonsen slowed and wound down the window as the man pointed at one of two trawlers moored at the dock. The hull was frozen into the ice.

"Hurry," the man said.

Simonsen drove along the dock and parked beside the second trawler, the one moored at the very edge of the dock. There were people on the deck, more men wearing factory overalls. A single woman was among them, hugging one of the men. She looked up as Simonsen climbed over the railings, pointing with one hand as she cradled the man's head with the other.

"Up there," she said.

Simonsen looked up, following the shrouds up the trawler's mast until he saw the body of a woman, neck bent, hanging from the last rung of the ladder welded to the mast. Simonsen cursed as he recognised the face of Oline Erngsen, her blue cheeks and enlarged eyes shone stiffly in the glare of the sodium lights mounted on the cabin. Simonsen knew then who the woman from the factory was consoling. He crossed the deck and laid a hand on Anton's shoulder.

"Come on, Anton," he said. "Let's get you inside." Simonsen stepped back as the woman guided Anton across the trawler deck. "Put him in my car," he said. "And stay with him."

Simonsen waited until he heard the click of the car door opening and shutting, before asking the three men from the factory to help him cut Oline down. Once they had her body on the deck, one of the men covered her with a tarpaulin as Simonsen called the hospital. His next call was to Gaba.

"I've got a suicide here, down by the docks," he said. "I'm going to be a while." He paused for a second. "You okay?"

The crackle of static on the line did little to disguise the rage in Gaba's voice, and Simonsen was impressed by the Sergeant's control.

"It's going to take some time," Gaba said. "Atii said she will stay and look at the video. I can't watch it again."

"I understand."

"I'll take Miki and Peter with Aqqa on the helicopter. But I'm sending Miki by himself to Marmoralik."

"The mine? Why?"

"We had another call since you left. The security guard at the mine said there was a polar bear busting into the huts. The guard was scared to go outside. So, we'll fly to the cabin and Miki can pick us up on the way back from the mine." Gaba paused. "I don't want to waste any time, Chief. The sooner we investigate the cabin, the sooner we can get back to work on the video. If we learn anything new at the cabin, it might open up some leads. We need to act on them as fast as possible."

"Okay," Simonsen said. "Keep me informed."

He ended the call and slipped his mobile into his pocket, just as a snow scooter slowed at the harbour entrance. Simonsen waved as he recognised Karl Nielsen from Inussuk. *Maratse's neighbour*, he recalled. Karl stopped on the ice below the deck of the trawler and Simonsen called down to him.

"Have you spoken to Maratse recently?" he asked.

"*Naamik.*"

"Have you seen him?"

"Not since the funeral."

"And you would tell me if you had?"

"Sure."

"Okay." Simonsen waved, as Karl accelerated away between the hulls of the smaller fishing boats frozen at their moorings.

He watched as Karl powered up the ramp onto the island and then drove along the road, past the hotel, until he lost sight of him up the hill between the Nukissiorfiit utility company local offices and the hospital. Once Karl was out of sight, Simonsen saw the ambulance leave the hospital. He walked back across the deck to hear the details surrounding Oline's death. Simonsen was pretty sure he knew why she had chosen to take her own life.

The hospital porter doubled as the ambulance driver. Simonsen helped him coordinate the men from the factory to lift Oline's body onto a stretcher. They carried her off the trawler to the back of the ambulance – a small transit van with a medical bag tucked beneath the driver's seat. One of the factory workers removed the tarpaulin. It crackled between his fingers as the porter draped a blanket over Oline's upper body.

"I'll be right along," Simonsen said, with a nod to the porter. He waited until the ambulance had turned and then opened the back seat of the police car. Simonsen climbed in beside Anton and took the man's hand. "I'm sorry," he said. "Do you want to go to the hospital?"

Anton shook his head. "Take me to my sister's."

"Okay."

Simonsen thanked the woman from the factory and then drove Anton along the docks and through the town. There was nothing Anton could do for

Oline, but at least he could be with family, those he had left. Simonsen struggled to link the different pieces of the puzzle surrounding Salik's murder and Petra's disappearance, but however they were linked – *if* they were linked at all – events were taking their toll on the people of Uummannaq. These were his people, his responsibility and they needed a break, a lead, anything to bring this to a close, and they needed it soon.

The tyres crunched into the drift of snow outside Anton's sister's house. Simonsen got out of the car, helped Anton out of the back seat, and supported him by the arm as they walked to the front door. He turned his head at the sound of a snow scooter braking as it came down the hill. It was Karl with a passenger. Simonsen wasn't sure, but in the few seconds it took for Karl to pass him, he thought he recognised the passenger as Natsi Hermansen.

Chapter 20

Maratse checked the dogs' feet, teasing clumps of ice from between their toes, running his fingers along the harnesses, frowning at the areas that had frayed a little and inspecting them closely as he clamped each dog between his knees and smoothed the ice from their canine beards when he was done with them. But the distractions didn't help; he couldn't erase Qitu's messages from his mind, especially the last one, the one that said Piitalaat was alive. Knowing it instead of just believing it, didn't make the waiting any easier, or the thudding of the second hand on his wrist any softer. Things were moving too slowly, and when the leads ended in dead ends and dead bodies, Maratse knew he couldn't continue without something stronger to work on.

He looked up at the sound of Karl's snow scooter approaching the old school house in Uummannatsiaq. Maratse waited by the dogs as Karl bumped the snow scooter from the ice to the land and stopped beside the schoolhouse. Karl told his passenger to wait inside, glancing at the hulk of an older snow scooter as he walked across the snow to shake Maratse's hand.

"He's a distant relation," Karl said, as he lit a cigarette. "The police raided his house. He knows people, David, but I don't think he'll tell you anything."

"We'll see."

"He's suspicious."

"*Iiji,*" Maratse said. He saw the young man stare at him from the schoolhouse window. "Did you take his mobile?"

"*Aap.*"

"Without a fuss?"

"Natsi is the son of my second cousin. He's scared I will tell his mother the truth about what he does for money."

"Scared enough to help me?"

"I don't know," Karl said. He blew a cloud of smoke from his lungs, noticing that Natsi had moved away from the window. "I think he's more frightened of the man who murdered Salik."

"Qitu thinks there is a connection."

"Who?"

"A journalist in Nuuk. Here," Maratse said, as he handed Karl his mobile.

"David," Karl said, as Maratse walked towards the schoolhouse. "What are you going to do?"

"Wait here."

"Maybe I should help."

The snow crunched beneath his boots as Karl took a step forwards. Maratse stopped him with a flat palm. He patted the older man softly on the chest.

"Stay here. Enjoy your cigarette. This won't take long."

Maratse let go of Karl and walked away.

"How do you know it won't take long?"

Maratse said nothing. He kicked the snow from his *kamikker* and stepped inside. The lantern lit the white walls with a flickering glow, casting shadows between the dark beams above the eating area of the kitchen. The tables had been pushed to one side. Maratse looked at Natsi as the young man perched at the end of a table, tapping the ends of his fingers as Maratse removed his mittens and tossed them onto the table opposite Natsi. He removed his anorak and the sealskin beneath it.

"It's warm in here," he said, as he rolled up the sleeves of his thermal top.

"No, man, it isn't," Natsi said.

"Man?"

"Yeah, *man*. You think you're some kind of hunter? Is that it? My dad's a hunter. The bastard."

"What's his name?" Maratse asked. He crossed the stone floor to the kitchen and picked up the dog whip from the counter. "Your father," he said. "What is his name?"

Natsi watched as Maratse coiled the whip into his fist. The sealskin cord was as wide as his thumb at the end that was bound tightly to a wooden shaft the length of Maratse's forearm. The cord tapered gradually over the six metre length until it was the same breadth and depth as the tip of his little finger.

"Why do you want to know?" Natsi swallowed as Maratse took a step towards him.

"Maybe I know him."

"I don't think so."

"Tell me anyway."

"No, man. I won't tell you anything."

Maratse dipped his head for a second as he gripped the coil and the first fist length of the shaft. The table creaked as Natsi took a step backwards.

"I'll call Karl."

"Karl is my friend."

Natsi slid along the table towards the door.

"He'll call the police if you touch me."

"I am the police," Maratse said.

"What?"

"Retired," he said, as he struck Natsi across the side of his face with the wooden shaft. Natsi fell to the floor and Maratse pinned him there as he looped a length of sealskin cord around both of Natsi's wrists. He cinched them tight, tossed the whip to one side of the room, and pulled the sealskin cord through an iron fitting bolted to the wall. Maratse dragged Natsi across the floor, tied the cord in a knot, and then pulled the cord attached to the opposite wall, stretching Natsi until he was on his knees, with his arms stretched tight. Natsi hunched forward with his shoulders just higher than his neck.

"Are you gonna hurt me, *man?*"

Maratse picked up the dog whip and placed it on the counter.

"There's nothing you can do to me that he hasn't done already." Natsi laughed as Maratse reacted to the word *he.* "You heard me. Salik had it coming. It was just sex for him, but the man – he wanted more. Salik should've known. He should've listened. Maybe he wouldn't be dead. Stupid, dumb *qaleralik.*" Natsi spat. "I had nothing to say to the police. I've got nothing to say to you."

Natsi twisted at the sound of the door opening.

"Karl," Maratse said. "Please leave."

Karl shook his head.

"I was thinking about it. I need to see this, if I am going to look his mother in the eye."

"You have to get out, Karl."

"Yeah, *old* man," Natsi said. "This party isn't for you. You don't have the stomach for it." He glared at Maratse. "And neither does he."

Maratse leaned over the counter and reached for a plastic bag. He placed it beside the whip. He ignored Natsi as he lifted a metal bucket of water from the kitchen floor and put it in front of Natsi.

"You're going to waterboard me, man?"

"You know what that is?"

"I've seen the movies. I'm not ignorant."

"Okay," Maratse said. He turned his back on Natsi and pulled the snow scooter battery from the bag. He put it on the floor next to the bucket of water and fiddled with two leads which he attached to the battery contacts. A spark flashed brighter than the lantern light, shining in Natsi's eyes and the young man paled.

"Hey," he said. His voice crackled and he coughed to clear it.

"You've seen the movies, Natsi," Maratse said. "So, you know what I am going to do with this, and the water. Right?" Maratse glanced at Karl. "You're sure you want to stay?"

Karl nodded.

Maratse kneeled in front of Natsi and gripped his chin. He pressed his face to within a few fingers of Natsi's face.

"I have a friend. She's in trouble," he said. Maratse tugged Natsi's chin and forced him to look at the battery and the water. "I would do anything to find her. I think your friend knows where she is. So, you're going to tell me where I can find him, or..."

"I can't tell you," Natsi whispered.

Maratse let go of Natsi's chin and stood up. He took a step back and peeled off his thermal top. He tossed it onto the table and picked up one of the lanterns. He held it close to his body and shone the light over his chest. Natsi stared at him. He swallowed as Karl let out a soft gasp.

"A Chinese man did this," Maratse said, as he traced the large blistered welts on his skin with his finger. "He used metal paddles with wooden handles. He had a generator. It was fast. The pain was intense, but quicker." Maratse lowered the lantern. He shined the light on the water and the battery. "This will take a lot longer."

Maratse lowered the lantern to the stone floor and kneeled again. He looked at Natsi as he picked up the leads and struck the ends to create another spark. There was a ladle in the bucket. Maratse filled it with water and splashed it over Natsi's head.

"David, wait," Karl said, as Maratse picked up the leads.

"I'm sorry, Karl. I don't think you'll be able to look in his mother's eyes."

"Wait," Natsi said.

"But we can start with the eyes," Maratse said. "Left or right, Natsi?"

"His name is Jaqqa Ujarneq," Natsi said. The water dribbled through his greasy hair. It spluttered from his lips as he spoke. "He's at the mine. He's always at the mine. That's where we go."

"What mine?" Maratse dipped the ladle into the water and lifted it.

"Marmoralik. The marble mine."

"He's there now?"

"*Aap.*"

"You're sure?"

"Yes, I'm sure."

Maratse tossed the ladle into the bucket and reached for his thermal top. He grabbed the dog whip from the counter and stepped over the cord securing Natsi's arm, stopping to pull on his sealskin.

"I'm coming with you," Karl said.

"*Eeqqi*," Maratse said, as he pulled the anorak

over his head. "But I need your snow scooter."

"What about the police?"

"Give me two hours, and then call them. You can take him back on the sledge."

"Two hours? What about Petra?"

"If he's there, he'll hear the helicopter. He'll kill her before they land."

"You don't know that."

"I can't risk it."

Maratse pressed the whip into Karl's hand and opened the door. Karl ran after him. He stopped by the snow scooter as Maratse slung his rifle over his chest and pulled a broad knife from beneath a cord on the sledge. He slid the knife between the bungee straps Karl had added to the snow scooter and climbed on.

"You were never going to hurt him," Karl said. "Were you?"

Maratse looked him in the eye as he turned the key in the ignition. The engine growled, belching a small cloud of smoke into the snow behind it.

"Not with a bucket of water and a scooter battery," Maratse said.

"But if he hadn't talked?"

"I would have used my bare hands," he said. Maratse revved the engine, pulled his ski mask over his head and nodded at Karl. "Two hours," he said.

Karl stepped back as the snow scooter lurched forwards. He watched Maratse until he reached the ice, and, losing sight of him as the snow scooter sped around the point of Uummannatsiaq, Karl turned back towards the schoolhouse, lit a cigarette and sat on the bench beside the front door and pictured Maratse tearing across the ice as he smoked. He wished he had made him promise to call or text if he needed help. Karl swore as he patted his pockets and realised Maratse had forgotten his mobile.

"Forgotten?" Karl whispered. "I wonder?"

It seemed unlikely. The more he got to know the retired Constable, the more he realised that despite his quiet and slow manner, there was little that Maratse forgot. The man was an enigma, and a thorn in the side of Uummannaq's Chief of Police. Despite all that had happened since Maratse had arrived in Inussuk, Karl liked his new neighbour.

He turned his head at a shout from Natsi. The thought crossed his mind that he could untie him.

"Two hours," he said, and lit another cigarette.

Chapter 21

The helicopter flared on the ridge above the cabin, the skids pressing into the snow covering the rocks as Gaba yanked the side door open and leaped out. Atii followed, with Danielsen and Peter jumping out of the other side. Miki waved from his seat next to the pilot and then the red Air Greenland Bell 212 lifted off in a white tempest, filling the folds and creases of the police officers' jackets and trousers with snow. Gaba waited until the snow had settled and the thunder of the rotor blades receded, before issuing his orders.

"Danielsen and Peter, I want you to work your way down to the ice," he said and pointed at the dark shape they had seen from the helicopter. "Atii and I will take the cabin. I want status updates on the radio every five minutes. Use your mobiles if there is interference." He gestured at the mountains. "The helicopter will be back in about thirty minutes. I want us on it within two hours."

Gaba waited for Danielsen to lead Peter down the mountainside, and then tapped Atii on the shoulder. He nodded as she tucked the MP5 into her shoulder and moved ten metres to his right. Despite the terrain she stuck to the distance as if they were connected with a length of elastic. Impressed, he nodded once and then worked his way off the ridge towards the cabin. The midday twilight gave plenty of light, enough to see that the cabin looked empty, with little sign of recent activity in the snow around it, other than a regular scuff of snow revealing old blood beneath it. Gaba stopped to inspect the first two scuffs. Despite the light layer of wind-blown snow covering it, he could see that it had been cleared with something about the size of his hand. Someone wearing mittens, perhaps. Atii scanned the area around the cabin as Gaba crouched by the blood. Someone had followed the trail either to or from the cabin.

"Maratse," he whispered.

A sudden gust of wind pressed beneath the lip of his ballistic helmet. Gaba tightened the straps, tugged the thin fleece hat beneath the helmet over his ears and waved for Atii to continue.

"Approaching the cabin," he said with a click of the radio attached to the shoulder of his bulletproof vest.

Atii moved in close, pressing her left hand on Gaba's shoulder as she aimed around him. Gaba opened the door, raised his MP5 and stepped quickly through the door frame. Atii followed, covering the right of the cabin as Gaba covered the left.

"Clear," she said.

"Clear." Gaba lowered his MP5 and let it hang on the strap cinched around his chest.

He tugged the small LED torch from his belt and lit the cabin with a powerful beam of light. Atii did the same. Starting from the ceiling, they searched the walls, the shelves, the furniture and the floor without taking another step. When Gaba saw something of interest on the floor he shone his light at it and Atii moved closer to investigate.

"Fish hooks and coloured thread," she said.

"Like on the boy's body."

"Sir?"

Atii's professionalism, regardless of their relationship, brought a thin smile to Gaba's face.

Coupled with her skill with the MP5 and the way she crossed the terrain and entered the cabin, Gaba decided she was a serious contender for Miki's role as his number two. *A little professional competition within the SRU is no bad thing*, he thought.

"Salik had fish hooks with coloured threads in the skin on his back." He pointed at the dust and ash beneath the stove with the beam of his torch. "If this is Aksel's cabin, or if he was here, we have a link to Salik's death right there."

Atii lit the mattress with her torch and pointed. "Condoms," she said. "Used."

"But not much else," Gaba said.

"Gaba?" Peter's voice crackled through the radio.

"Go ahead."

"We've found Aksel's body. Danielsen has identified him."

"Dead?"

"A rifle bullet in the head. He's naked. His clothes have been tossed around the ice. Danielsen says it looks just like Sergeant Jensen's crime scene. The place where she committed suicide."

"Supposedly."

"*Aap.*"

"Okay. Start documenting the scene. Oh, and Peter?"

"*Aap.*"

"Tell Danielsen to call it in to the Chief."

Gaba pulled out his phone and started taking pictures of the cabin interior. Atii did the same, starting with the hooks and thread, the condoms, even the magazines on the shelves. Gaba pulled on a pair of thin plastic gloves and collected the fish hooks into a clear plastic bag. He tucked it into the chest pocket of his vest, and found another bag for the condoms.

"If this was Aksel and Salik's love nest," he said, as he sealed the condoms inside the evidence bag, "we can start joining the dots."

"What about Aksel? The rifle bullet in his head..."

"Could be Maratse's. He's mirrored what happened to Petra."

"You mean Aksel did that to Petra?" Atii pointed at the condoms as Gaba secured the bag inside another pocket. "It doesn't make sense, if Aksel was screwing Salik. Why would he take Petra?"

"Danielsen said they found photos on Salik's computer. I want you to look at them when we get back. Compare them with this place," Gaba said. He checked the signal on his phone and swore. "How's your phone?"

"No service."

"Miki was supposed to call." Gaba pressed the transmit button on his radio. "Peter, any word from Miki?"

"He's at the mine. He was just about to meet with the security guard. The helicopter is on its way back." Peter paused. "I think I can hear it."

"Right. Tidy up the scene and cover the body. You can't carry it up the mountain. Simonsen can arrange to have it picked up later." Gaba nodded at Atii. "We're leaving."

They moved quickly through the snow to the ridge above the cabin, sheltering just beneath the ridge as the helicopter landed. Their breath clouded the interior of the helicopter as they waited for Danielsen and Peter to return from the ice.

"Did you see the bear?" Gaba asked the pilot.

"We did a circle of the mine. Saw some damage to some of the huts. Your officer..."

"Miki."

"Right. He said to leave him there. The security guard had a rifle. He said they would be fine."

Gaba nodded and then opened the door for Danielsen and Peter. The pilot started the engines, and the helicopter whined and shuddered into life. The view through the windows was obscured in a cloud of white needles until the pilot took off and they escaped the snow on the mountain. Normally, Gaba might have enjoyed the view of the moonlight lighting the snowy peaks of the mountains. He would have looked as the pilot pointed out the coloured houses and buildings of the settlement of Saattut, or marvelled at the way the twin peaks of Uummannaq mountain really did look heart-shaped, just before the helicopter slowed to a hover above the landing pad. But the job wasn't done, they hadn't found Petra, and the one man they wanted to question was dead.

Convenient, he thought, as the pilot settled the helicopter on the landing pad and shut down the engines. Gaba was the first out of the door, striding across the pad towards Simonsen and the police car parked at the heliport gates.

"Aksel is dead," Gaba said, as he tossed his helmet and vest into the boot of the police car.

"How?"

"Rifle bullet to the head. Danielsen has the photos. You'll need to pick up the body."

"Later," Simonsen said. He watched as Danielsen and the SRU officers removed their helmets. "You're corrupting my Constable, Sergeant," he said, with a nod at Danielsen. "Don't fill his head with gung ho

SRU delusions. I need him here."

Gaba shrugged and climbed into the passenger seat. He started giving orders as soon as everyone was inside and Simonsen pulled away from the gates.

"Danielsen and Atii, I want you to go through all the photos. Peter will start processing the physical evidence."

"Lucky for you," Atii said and thumped Peter on the arm.

"I'll check in with Nuuk."

"No need," Simonsen said, as he slowed to a stop outside the hotel. "Your tech guy called. They've processed the video, the audio. About the only thing linking the video to Greenland is Sergeant Jensen." Simonsen turned off the engine. "She's still alive," he said. "The Commissioner has agreed to buy another ten minutes of video, but he's waiting for confirmation from Denmark. The tech team there is also on the case." Simonsen paused and looked at his watch. "The media have got wind of the story. There's a press conference scheduled for about twenty minutes from now."

"Press conference?" Gaba said, as he got out of the car.

"Live. Together with the First Minister. I've got a television set up in the dining room."

Gaba excused himself as his team sorted the gear and Danielsen briefed Simonsen on what they had found on the ice. He heard Simonsen curse as he pounded up the stairs to his room. Gaba realised he didn't care if Maratse had killed Aksel, what bothered him, what really pissed him off, was the thought that Maratse knew something, and that he was withholding information that could help them find

Petra.

"Why?" he said, as he stared into the bathroom mirror.

Gaba called Miki, frowning as the call was diverted to voicemail. He finished up in the bathroom and joined the team in the dining room just as the *KNR* news anchor announced the start of the press conference. Gaba recognised the line-up, with Nivi Winther standing beside the Commissioner and Malik Uutaaq.

"What's he doing there?"

"He's pegged for a ministerial post," Simonsen said with a shrug. "I don't understand either."

"Who's the girl standing next to Qitu? The one with the pink hair?"

"No idea."

Gaba listened as the Commissioner explained the situation concerning the disappearance of Sergeant Petra Jensen. He fielded questions regarding her supposed suicide, before deferring to the First Minister. She introduced Qitu and talked about an ongoing investigation into an underground culture of sex and violence. Then she beckoned Qitu to the microphone.

"Gaba," Atii said.

"In a minute."

"You'll want to see this now," she said and placed a hand on his arm.

"See what?" Gaba followed Atii to where Danielsen sat at the computer.

"These are the photos from Salik's computer." Atii tapped the screen. "This is the window in the photos. We've cleaned it up as best we can. Do you see the line stretching from one side to the other?"

"Yes."

"It's on all of the photos. The same window. The line is too thick to be a washing line, or a rope. It looks more like a cable."

"At an angle?"

"*Aap.*" Atii waited as Simonsen joined them. "These are Salik's photos. We're pretty sure he was involved in some kind of extreme sex or violent acts. They need somewhere private for that."

"Like the cabin," Gaba said and leaned closer to the screen.

"*Aap.* But there's only one window in Aksel's cabin, and no cable outside."

"There's all kinds of cables and wires in the settlements," Danielsen said. "On boats and hanging from cranes."

"In Nuuk too," Atii said.

"But they usually hang straight down," Danielsen said. "This one is at an angle. It looks like it is pretty far away, but it's still thick."

"Tell me what it is, Constable." Gaba rapped the table with his knuckle.

"I think it's the cable for a cable car," he said. "And if it's in this area, then there's only one place it can be."

"Marmoralik mine," Simonsen said.

Gaba swore and pulled out his mobile. "We need the helicopter," he said with a look at Simonsen. He swore again when he heard the voicemail message on Miki's phone.

"Just a second," Simonsen said. "Even if Salik and friends were at the mine, how do we know Sergeant Jensen might be there?"

"It's deserted in the winter," Danielsen said.

"There's just one guard for the whole winter. He lives there."

"Do we have a name?"

"Jaqqa Ujarneq."

"What?" Simonsen said, as Karl walked into the dining room.

"The guard's name is Jaqqa. He's at the mine now. Maratse told me to tell you."

"Maratse?" Simonsen gripped the back of Danielsen's chair.

"And where is Maratse now?" Gaba said.

"He's on his way to the mine." Karl looked at his watch. "He should be there by now."

"And so is Miki," Gaba said. He clicked his fingers at Peter. "Gear up," he said. "Everyone, now."

Chapter 22

The plates in the sink rattled and the walls of the cabin shook. Petra rubbed at her eyes and stared around the room. The grey light behind the curtains drew her out of the bed and she wrapped the sheet around her as she walked across the floor. The rattling increased as a familiar *thud thud thud* triggered a rush of adrenalin through her body. It spread like fire to her fingertips, the ink bands in the joints of her fingers pulsed with energy and, for the moment at least, she ignored the ache in her hips, the sore patches of skin and the stiffness in her muscles. She pressed warm fingers to her lips and almost smiled at the touch. Petra drew back the curtain and saw the big red helicopter descend to the landing pad. She struggled to take it all in – the helicopter, the cabins, and the tube-like metal cab hanging from a thick cable. The orange paint on the cab was blistered like her lips.

The helicopter's blades thundered just beyond the cabins. Petra looked around the room for her clothes – any clothes. She considered running out in the sheet, but anything more than a walk turned the warmth in her body to fiery needles, slowing her down. Perhaps the helicopter would wait? But the rattling of the plates increased as did the pitch of the rotor blades, as the Air Greenland helicopter lifted up and away from the landing pad. She glimpsed the bottom of it as it passed the window.

Petra gripped the window sill, pressed her head against the cool pane of glass, and felt the adrenaline seep out of her body. She started to shake as her body chilled. She should have run to the helicopter.

I can't. My legs, my muscles, everything hurts.

She should have tried at least while she had the chance.

Petra felt the sheet slip from her shoulders. She grabbed at it, caught a corner in her fingers, and winced as a broken nail was tangled in the threads. And then her knees buckled and she slid down the wall to the floor, her hand slipping from the windowsill, as the distant roar of the helicopter diminished and she was alone again.

But I'm not alone, she thought.

Her body shook with a sudden rush of fear.

Did he leave on the helicopter? Was she alone? And what about them?

What if the man left her alone with them, the ones who forced him to do what he did to her? If she was truly alone, then who would stop them? Who would set her free?

"He promised," she whispered, as she looked at her banded fingers. Petra clenched one fist and thumped it softly against the wall. "He promised."

She looked back at the bed; saw the camera on its tripod and the glow of the screen pointing towards her, the lens fixed on the mattress. They were still here, watching, forcing him to do the things that hurt. Would he hurt her if they didn't tell him to?

"No," she whispered. "He's sick. And now he's gone."

The air between the cabins sank in the wake of the helicopter, and, as it settled, the wind began to chatter, gusting shouts at the glass, brushing words against the cabin walls. Petra pressed her ear against the wall, catching her hair in the flecks and splinters in the wood. The wooden wall amplified the voices until she could understand the words, Danish with the occasional Greenlandic exclamation.

"It was over there."

Petra's heart spasmed with an extra beat at the sound of *his* voice. *He's still here*, she thought.

"Just stand still for a minute. Let it come to us."

The second voice was familiar, but distant, as if she knew it once, but couldn't place it. And then it was gone, hidden beneath a bestial huffing and the crash of metal. An oil drum, perhaps? Petra reached for the windowsill and pulled herself onto her knees. The energy she felt when the noise from the helicopter had tugged her out of bed had been sapped with the roller coaster emotions of abandonment and fear. But the voices, two of them, gave her just enough energy to peer out through the window, past the ice flowers decorating the inside of the glass. Petra scraped at the flowers, pressing a film of ice beneath her broken fingernails. She made a hole, enough for one eye to see the space between the cabins, the man with a hunting rifle in his hands, and a second man, wearing black. Her brow creased as she tried to process a burst of familiarity – there was something about his jacket, the black trousers, and black boots. She knew this man. Not as well as some, but enough to realise he was important. He could help her.

"Hey," she said. She cleared her throat and tried again, a spot of blood bursting beneath the scab on her lips as she tried to shout. "Hey."

Petra tried to knock on the window. If felt loud in the confines of the cabin, but not loud enough to compete with the huffing of the beast and the shouts of the men. She saw it then, a large bear, ranging towards the man in black. She shuddered at the *crack*

crack of the weapon in the man's hand. She saw the burst of orange flame from the barrel. Petra heard the bear roar. And then there were more cracks, and a loud bang. She saw a puff of smoke cling to the air around *his* head. She heard the other man's voice.

"Wait there," he said.

Petra watched him walk towards the bear, the gun in his hands tucked tight into his shoulder, the muzzle pointing at the bear lying on the ground, its creamy fur striped with deep red blood, like rust. Petra heard the snick of the rifle as *he* worked the bolt and aimed at the bear. He was helping the other man, she was sure of it. And then he pulled the trigger and the man in black slumped onto the bear.

Petra couldn't breathe. She didn't feel the frost on the window cooling her fingers, or the soft scratch of the sheet as it slipped from her shoulders. She watched him walk towards the man in black and drag his body off the top of the bear. Then she saw him struggle, lifting the bear's head with one hand as he tried to drag the man in black beneath it, just his head, so that when he let go of the bear, its jaw covered the dead man's head. The man pointed the rifle at the bear's head, adjusted the angle, and then fired again. Then he turned towards the cabin, fiddling with something he had strapped to his head as he slung the rifle over his shoulder and walked towards the cabin. Petra heard him kick the snow from his boots and then he opened the door.

"You're up," he said, as he leaned the rifle against the wall and removed his outer clothes. "I thought you were going to sleep all day."

Petra clung to the wall. She watched him as he removed the camera from the strap around his head and placed it on the counter in the kitchen area. He filled the kettle with water, watching her as it bubbled and spat. Petra said nothing. She didn't move. She just watched him. The man made two mugs of tea. He placed one in front of her and then drew up a chair. He nodded towards the window.

"You saw what happened?" He sipped his tea. "It's okay," he said. "Tragic, really, but that's what they wanted." He turned to point at the camera on the counter. "It's a GoPro camera. High Definition but no sound." He shrugged. "It's probably best without the sound. They'll have to use their imagination."

"Who was he?"

"Him? He was a policeman, Petra. Oh," he said, nodding his head. "Perhaps you knew him. I don't know his name. I just called and asked for help with the bear. Of course, I could have killed it with the rifle, but since working with you, well... I realised there is a lot of money to be made when working with the police. So, I asked for help." He rested his arms on his knees and warmed his hands around the mug. "Now, I admit, it's a little risky. Bit of a game changer, but the game has to change if we want to make the big bucks, as they say."

"I don't understand."

"Of course not. Um, let me think," he said, and paused. "Things are moving quite fast, and you'll soon be free." He pointed at her hands. "And as we've only got a short time together now, I may as well explain a few things. First, just so we're clear, I never realised how much people hate the police. I mean, they," he said, and pointed at the camera on the tripod, "they want to see people like you get hurt.

They'll pay for it. I've got enough money put aside now for a good long time. But, now we have to step things up a gear. We have to move fast."

He sipped his tea, watching Petra over the rim, his eyes flicking from her hair to her shoulders, to her bare chest, her skin cooling, goose bumping.

"It won't be long before they come," he said. "They'll see that it was an accident, that the bear attacked that poor policeman and that I tried my best to kill the bear, but I missed." He held up two fingers. "Twice. It is tragic and there will be consequences. I'll be charged of course, but..." He shrugged. "A fine. Manslaughter at the very worst. But we have to clear up all this," he said with a wave that took in the whole room.

He coughed, pressed the back of his hand to his mouth, and looked at the blood speckling his skin. Petra shivered as she watched him.

"It's TB," he said. "I didn't know Salik was sick." The man sighed as he wiped the blood from his hand on his trousers. He pulled a coloured thread from his pocket and twisted it around his finger. "He's free now, though, Salik. I thought I loved him. You know what I mean? It's complicated, but I had to let him go. It became too personal, too much to handle. It's so much easier with you," he said. "Of course, I should thank you too. Without you I wouldn't have been able to set Salik free."

Petra wrapped her arms around her chest and pressed her fingers into her skin. She tried to stop the shivering, tried to control her tongue, to form the words, to ask about her freedom. The man smiled, as if he knew what she wanted to ask.

"It's all planned," he said. "Every detail. Do you

want to hear it?"

"Yes," Petra whispered.

"Well," he said and stood up. He walked to the camera and turned it off. He opened a packet of batteries and replaced the dead ones in the camera as he talked. "It's genius really, but to start from the beginning. I took you from Uummannaq. Do you remember? You travelled with Salik on the sledge."

Petra caught the image of the young man, his face pressed against hers beneath the tarpaulin.

"You see, Salik died. Very sad, very unfortunate, but fact. I knew people had seen me with Salik, but they didn't know he had been with someone else too. An old man," he said and sneered. "They thought I didn't know, but I know everything. I even filmed it. Not for money, you understand. I filmed it because I had to. It was all part of the plan. I left the camera with the old man's body. He's free too. Do you see? I freed Salik, and I freed the old man. But you have freed me, because you gave me the chance to walk away."

"How?"

He picked up the GoPro camera and sat down, replacing the batteries as he talked. "I was in town the day the old man – Aksel – had a run-in with your friend, the retired policeman. What was his name?"

Petra tried to remember. The shivering stopped as a deeper cold settled on her body, pressing her into the floor as she realised she had lost time, had forgotten things, she had forgotten him. But the cold grip seemed to squeeze a new resolve from sudden hidden depths, and she saw him again, all in white, just the eyes – those soft brown eyes – she could see them, and she knew his name.

"David," she said.

"That's right. Constable David Maratse." The man laughed. "When I heard about their confrontation, I knew Maratse would not forget Aksel. And then it all clicked into place. Once Salik was free, I took you because I knew your Maratse would come looking for you, and that he would start with Aksel. With the video and those awful fish hooks, well... the police are so predictable. They will link Salik's death with Aksel. When they find Aksel's body, they will assume Maratse killed him – an act of revenge, you see. For you." He paused to close the camera case. "Now, we really must hurry, because I have heard that your friend has discovered where you are."

Petra pressed her hand over her mouth. The shivering stopped.

"Oh," he said. "That pleases you? Well, that's good. Of course, the poor policeman outside, he is insurance, you see. When I heard the bear I realised I had another play to make. Maratse will come looking for you; the police will come looking for their colleague." He stood up and walked to the bed. He lifted the mattress and pulled out a ski suit, socks and a hat. "I can see some of the details puzzle you," he said, as he dumped the clothes on the floor beside Petra. "The bullet in Aksel's brain isn't from just any rifle. Do you know Karl? I took his rifle last week and returned it when I was finished with it. Maratse's rifle is old and I knew he would borrow Karl's. So, the evidence is planted, along with the motive. Now we just have to see who comes first? Maratse or the police. But you'd better get dressed. We have to go into the mine. It's time to set you free."

Chapter 23

Maratse turned off the engine and let the snow scooter drift to a halt on the sea ice, two hundred metres from Marmoralik mine. He stepped off the snow scooter and felt the wind beat at his anorak. It was nothing compared to the wind blasting his cheeks on the ride across the fjord. He pressed his fingers around his face, felt the hard skin, the flesh solid to his touch. Maratse lifted the seat, wrapped a wire around the battery and bound it around the handle next to the start switch. He removed the rubber grip with his knife. Once he was finished, he studied the living quarters, the mess hall, the satellite dish and the office buildings clustered around the base of the mine, right beside the helicopter landing pad. It had passed him as he sped across the fjord. He had seen it again on its return, just ten minutes later. He was curious as to who might have visited the mine, concerned that they might cause problems. The second hand thumped from his watch into his wrist. He took it off and fastened it around the handlebars of the snow scooter. Time was of little consequence now. He had arrived, and now he had to act.

Maratse tugged the rifle from his chest and worked a bullet into the chamber. He left his mittens on the seat of the snow scooter and tugged the silk ski mask onto his forehead, like a hat. Maratse crossed his arms, hugging the rifle to his chest as he walked across the ice towards the rocks below the mine.

Close to the rocky shore the ice was soft, and Maratse slowed to pick a dry route onto the land. He skipped onto a small floe of ice bobbing in the water, and then further onto the land, holding the rifle in one hand as he grasped a pointed rock with the other. He paused for a moment, studied the light and wondered if he should wait until it was dark. A quick glance at the halogen lamps scattered around the buildings suggested it wouldn't matter either way. If Jaqqa decided to turn them on.

Jaqqa. He had a name but no history, no motive. But none of that mattered. This man had Piitalaat. He was sure of it. It had to be right; this had to be the place. She had to be here. He felt the weight of the rifle in his hands and wondered what he would do if she wasn't. Could he live without her? Would he even try?

"No time for that" he said and climbed up the rocks to the accommodation block.

The area was flat, blasted smooth with rubble around the perimeter. The cabins linked with insulated wires and pipes. Empty oil drums covered in dents and rust – the ubiquitous gargoyles of the High Arctic – gathered in groups, or stood alone, beside cabins. The oil drums peopled the deserted mine with stoic figures, some painted, others naked, bitten into splinters by the frost and the wind, shadows of the last human activity before the onset of winter. Maratse worked his way around the cabins, until he saw the bear.

Maratse paused at the sight of it, saw the body – head tucked beneath the bear's jaw – and scanned the surrounding buildings. The windows were dusted and flowered with ice. No witnesses. No-one watching. Maratse walked to the bear and kneeled beside the body. He shoved the bear's head to one side and sighed as he recognised Miki, the young SRU officer. Maratse wasn't much for riddles or games. He preferred the more straightforward cases – someone missing and needing to be found, an opportunistic but typically dumb robbery, even a drunken brawl. But this, like the body of Aksel on the ice, naked with clothes strewn to all sides, it suggested a plan of sorts. A scheme within which he had a part to play; and he had to play by rules that he didn't understand, rules that changed the minute Jaqqa had taken Piitalaat. He must have known that. And if he didn't then, he must surely know now.

The bark and shudder of a large diesel generator startled Maratse away from the bear and Miki's body, as he moved behind an oil drum and scanned the buildings for movement.

Nothing.

Only the generator, and then the grind of a large cable around a drum. An orange capsule, like a small bus without wheels, swung into view as it rose up from behind the cabins and ticked along the wire towards the dock bolted to the mountainside above the camp. There were two faces in the windows. Maratse ignored the man, and focused on the woman instead.

"Piitalaat," he said and stood up.

She pressed a small hand against the window as the man gripped her by the hair and lifted her head. Maratse saw the barrel of a rifle pressed into the soft skin beneath her chin. He held his breath until the cable car stopped at the dock above, and Jaqqa forced Petra onto the rocks leading into the entrance of the mine. Maratse started to pick a route between the rocks, wondering if he could climb so high, if his legs would finally give up the charade of overcoming his previous injuries, and simply quit working on the rocks, failing him and failing Petra.

Maratse slung the rifle around his chest and jogged to the rock face. He stopped at the sound of the cable car lurching away from the dock with a metallic thud, ticking down the cable towards the camp. It was part of the game, Maratse realised. The grander scheme. Jaqqa wanted him to play his part.

Maratse waited for the empty cable car to swing to a stop and opened the door. He gripped the handle, pausing for a moment at the sound of something beating against the wind, somewhere in the distance, beyond the fjord. It could have been a helicopter. If Karl had given his message, then it was probably the police. If Miki was here, then the chances of Gaba and his team being on the helicopter was high.

I should wait, he thought. But the next thought was of Petra and Maratse closed the door.

Jaqqa had left a trail from the cable car dock leading into the mine. If it hadn't been for the sight of Petra, Maratse might have stopped to consider what it meant, what Jaqqa intended to do. Maratse ignored the fish hooks hammered into the wooden rails. The brightly coloured threads twisted in the wind, losing momentum and colour, sapped of energy the closer Maratse got to the entrance of the mine. The air inside the mine was denser, it lay thick in the entrance, like treacle tugging at Maratse's *kamikker*, and clinging to the thick hairs of his polar bear skin trousers. Maratse peered into the mine, found a long thread attached to the last of the hooks and teased it between his fingers as he followed it inside.

"I knew you would come." Jaqqa's voice echoed around the walls.

"Why?"

"It was just a matter of time."

"Hm," Maratse said, as he followed the thread deeper into the mine.

"We've been waiting for you," Jaqqa said. "And now you're here."

Maratse reached the end of the thread. He stopped as it slipped through his fingers. Something clicked to his right and then a powerful beam blinded him as Jaqqa turned on the interior lights.

"Welcome to Marmoralik," Jaqqa said, his voice loud, theatrical, the words echoing up the walls, curving around the low ceiling. "Smile for the camera, Constable Maratse."

Maratse crumpled to the rocky floor as a bullet slammed into his thigh. The boom of the rifle repeated like a machine gun, but only one bullet hit Maratse. The polar bear hairs of his trousers turned crimson in the harsh light and he winced at the pain. It was deep, but Petra's scream went deeper still, lancing through his body like a harpoon, the tip breaking off as she drew another breath. Maratse shielded his eyes and scrabbled on the floor for his rifle.

"Self-defence," Jaqqa said. "That's what they'll say. You were armed. You rushed to attack me, while I tried to defend this young woman, to protect her from you."

"What about Miki?"

"Who's Miki?"

"The policeman you shot by the bear," Maratse said.

"More self-defence. An unfortunate accident. I have it all on film. Step closer Maratse. I want to show you something."

Maratse stumbled towards the light, with slow steps. They reminded him of that time, after the Chinese man, when he had forced himself to walk, and Petra had taught him to live again. She was here. She was alive. Just past the lights.

But Petra wasn't behind the lights, she was above them.

Maratse used the rifle as a crutch and looked up at a small gantry. He could see Petra's feet, he could almost reach them. Her hands were tied, her mouth gagged. Jaqqa stood beside her on the gantry, one hand on the railing and the other tugging the noose above Petra's head.

"We faked it last time," he said. "This time it should be real."

"I don't understand," Maratse said.

"No? Look at her fingers. I'm going to set her free."

There was blood on Petra's thumbs, dark, like ink.

"And if you look over there," Jaqqa said and pointed to a second gantry. "Look at the camera. I left an iPad at the entrance; it's all connected to a satellite phone. Expensive, but don't worry, it's all covered. I remember someone once said you have to make as much money as you can, when you can. Well, the time is now, Maratse. And this is the end. You might think I am a demon, but I'm just a storyteller. My viewers – they gave me the script, they told me what to do." Jaqqa coughed. He wiped the blood from his hand on Petra's ski suit. "Petra knows that. She understands."

"Piitalaat," Maratse said, as he caught her eye. He

lowered his rifle. "It's going to be okay."

Petra's eyes, wide and black in the dark, stared back at Maratse. Her feet twitched as Jaqqa tugged at the noose, her socks sliding on the gantry's wooden plank.

"It's touching, of course, but it's all part of the plan." Jaqqa nodded at the camera. "It's a real cliffhanger, if you'll pardon the pun."

"I'm going to help you, Piitalaat."

"Oh, I'm counting on it," Jaqqa said. "As soon as I let her go." He kissed Petra on the cheek and brushed the hair from her eyes. "You really were wonderful to work with. *Qujanaq*," he said, and pushed her over the edge.

Maratse slipped as he leaped, cursing the wound in his leg as he gripped Petra's legs, pressed his hands beneath her heels and lifted her feet. She twisted above him, bumping against the side of the gantry, fingers splayed, mouth open. Petra gasped as the noose tightened and Maratse stumbled beneath her. Jaqqa hovered in front of them. He steadied the GoPro camera on his head as he circled them, laughing once as he retreated down the mine towards the entrance.

Maratse grunted with the pain from his leg and the weight of Petra above him. It wasn't her bodyweight that he struggled with; it was the thought of letting go, of losing her that bore down on him.

"I won't let go," he said. "Not ever."

His leg twitched with the effort, and Maratse began to wonder just how deep the wound was. Was this how it would end? Petra hanging at the end of a rope as Maratse bled to death beneath her?

"You are free," Jaqqa shouted from the mine

entrance. "Both of you."

Chapter 24

The slow moving high pressure air beneath the rotor blades of the helicopter pushed the aircraft into the faster, low pressure air above, as Gaba clicked the microphone on his headset and read the email on his phone to his team. The pilot dipped the helicopter's nose and increased speed towards the mine at Marmoralik.

"Jaqqa Ujarneq," Gaba said, "is twenty-eight years old. He was born in Denmark. Lived most of his life just outside Copenhagen. He moved back to Greenland two years ago. His circle of friends in Denmark includes a hacker and others known to the police. The tech teams in Nuuk and Denmark believe Jaqqa may have had help from his hacker friend, and other associates, to set up and access the tech needed to stream and sell his videos." Gaba slipped his phone into his pocket. "Honestly, we don't care about that. We know he is an evil son-of-a-bitch and we are going to take him down today. The email from Nuuk suggested he has some mental health issues which make it difficult for him to empathise with people." He turned in the co-pilot's seat to look at Atii, Peter and Danielsen sitting on the seats behind the cockpit. "Let's be clear about this. There's no sympathy or empathy from us today. We find Petra and then we take him down. He stays alive until she is found. If we plug him, I don't care if we have to set up an on-the-spot blood transfusion, he stays alive. As long as he can talk then he can tell us where she is. We'll let the detectives in Nuuk find out the rest. Are we clear?"

"Clear," Atii said.

Peter nodded.

"Danielsen?" Gaba tapped him on the knee. "You understand?"

"*Aap.*"

"Simonsen didn't want you to come. He thinks you're easily impressed by this," Gaba said with a wave at the two heavily-armed and armoured SRU officers sitting either side of Danielsen. "He thinks we might be a bad influence. Is he right?"

"Yes, Sergeant."

"Good," Gaba said and smiled.

"What about Miki?" Atii asked. "We haven't heard from him."

"I know," Gaba said. "Something's not right. What I said before, about keeping Jaqqa alive – obviously, that applies to Miki too."

"Two minutes," the pilot said.

"Peter, you're our medic. Danielsen stays with you."

"Got it."

"Atii?"

"*Aap?*"

"You're on point. I'll be right behind you. According to the map we've got thirty buildings to search. That will take time. We stack-up outside each building, Atii first, me second, Peter third, and Danielsen stays outside. Every time. Same procedure. Each building."

Gaba paused as the pilot turned into a slow circle above the mine. Atii was the first to spot the polar bear and the dark shape partly obscured beneath it. She called it out and pointed.

"Over there," the pilot said. "The cable car is moving."

"There's a man inside," Peter said.

"Put us down now," Gaba said, as he unbuckled his seat belt. "New plan," he said, with a quick look at his team. "Move fast to the cable car and surround it."

"What about Miki?" Atii asked. "That could be him under the bear."

"Danielsen checks him on the way, the rest of us move, move move."

Gaba opened the door as Atii and Peter slid open the side doors. The helicopter skids barely kissed the ice on the landing pad as Gaba leaped out and ran up the narrow road towards the cable car. He heard Atii's light step to his right, and the heavier pounding of Peter's boots behind him. Gaba ran right past the bear and the body beneath it. That was Danielsen's responsibility. The rest of the team had only one objective: secure the cable car and the occupants before they could get out, or start the return journey back to the mine.

"On the ground," Gaba shouted as a man opened the sliding door of the cable car. "Now," he said, as he slowed, MP5 extended, the sling taut, and the sights trained on a man with a small camera strapped to his head.

"I give up," the man said.

"Jaqqa Ujarneq?"

"Yes."

"Get on the ground." Gaba closed the gap, circling Jaqqa as he walked towards the cable car. "Atii?"

"Got him," she said, as she slammed her knees into Jaqqa's back.

Peter covered her with his MP5 as Gaba entered the cable car.

"He's secure," he said, as Gaba came out again.

"Get him up."

Jaqqa grunted as Atii and Peter pulled him onto his knees. Atii gripped the ties binding his hands behind his back and lifted his arms, forcing Jaqqa to swear as Gaba stood in front of him and gripped him by the chin. Gaba waited until Danielsen joined them. He swore when Danielsen nodded.

"It's Miki," he said.

Atii swore and gripped Jaqqa's hair, pulling back his head as Gaba leaned closer.

"Jaqqa Ujarneq," Gaba said. "Where is Sergeant Petra Jensen?"

"Aren't you going to arrest me?" Jaqqa asked. "Don't you have to look at your watch and say the time, and..." he paused to cough and Gaba let go of his chin and stepped back as Jaqqa spat a stream of blood onto the snow. "You have to arrest me."

"Why?" Atii asked.

"Then I'll be in your custody."

"You already are," she said.

Jaqqa twisted to look at her. "You have to make it official."

"Jaqqa Ujarneq," Gaba said.

"Yes?"

Gaba raised his hand and slapped Jaqqa across the mouth, splitting Jaqqa's lip and smearing blood on his glove. Gaba made a show of looking at his watch. "The time is 16:34, and you are under arrest for the kidnapping and torture of a police officer, amongst many, many other things."

"What things?"

Gaba hit him again. He pressed his fingers around Jaqqa's throat and lifted him onto his feet, turning him to look down the short road to the landing pad.

"That man," he said and pointed at Miki, "was a good friend of mine. You had something to do with his death. I'll find that out later. Right now, you're going to tell me where Petra is."

"You're too late."

"No," Gaba said. "That's not the right answer." He kicked Jaqqa's knees and dropped him to the ground. Gaba shifted his grip to Jaqqa's hair and pulled his head back. "Try again."

"I said you're too late. She'll be dead already. They both will."

"Who?"

"Maratse and your Sergeant. They're in the mine."

"Peter," Gaba said, as he kicked Jaqqa onto the ground. "Watch him."

Atii and Danielsen followed Gaba into the cable car. Gaba pushed the button to climb back up the mountain as Danielsen closed the door.

"Miki?" he asked.

"He was shot twice. Once through the bear. Maybe the bear caught him by surprise?"

"Unlikely." Gaba tapped his leg. "Come on, come on."

Atii was the first out of the cable car. Gaba and Danielsen ran after her, faster when they heard her shout. Gaba watched her climb the gantry and ordered Danielsen to help her as he ran to Maratse. He was at least a head taller than the retired Constable, and he gripped Petra's legs, shoving them straight up as Maratse slumped against him.

"Cut her down, Atii," Gaba shouted.

He looked up at Petra, saw the gag in her mouth. Her hair covered her eyes. He couldn't see if they were open.

"We have to pull her up," Danielsen said.

"Do it." Gaba lifted her feet, pushing her soles above his head as Danielsen and Atii pulled her up and over the side of the gantry. "Status?"

"Unconscious. We've got a pulse. Slow, thready," Atii said. "She's breathing."

Gaba sank to his knees and gripped Maratse by the shoulder. "She's breathing," he said. "She's okay."

"*Iiji.*"

"What about you?"

"I'm okay."

"You're bleeding." Gaba lay Maratse down and inspected the blood pooling in the hairs of the polar bear skin trousers. He pulled a folding knife from his utility belt. "I have to take a look," he said.

"*Eeqqi,*" Maratse said, and placed a hand on Gaba's arm. "Buuti will kill me."

"She can blame me," Gaba said, and grinned.

Maratse lay down as Gaba slipped the tip of the knife into the hole torn by the bullet. He cut a patch in the trousers and tossed the bloody patch of bearskin to one side.

"Piitalaat?" Maratse said.

"She's alright," Gaba said. "We'll get her down in a second." He looked up at the gantry. "I need some bandages," he said.

"Danielsen," Atii said, as she removed the noose from Petra's neck. "Bandages in the back of my vest."

Gaba caught the bandages from Danielsen and continued to cut away at the trousers. When he could see the entry and exit wound, he rolled Maratse onto his side, pressed the dressing over the wound and bound it tight.

"We'll get a stretcher. Danielsen will stay with you."

"I can walk," Maratse said.

"I know you can, but..."

"I'll walk."

Gaba nodded. "You're a stubborn bastard."

"*Iiji.*"

"Rest for a minute. I'm going to help them with Petra."

The ladder to the top of the gantry was thin with rusted rungs. Gaba climbed halfway as Danielsen and Atii lowered Petra into his arms. She was lighter than he remembered, thinner, her skin bruised, black in places. Gaba gripped her body with one arm, and with her head over his shoulder, he climbed down the ladder. Maratse helped him at the bottom, peeling Petra from Gaba's arms as he lowered her onto the ground. Gaba stepped back as Maratse pulled Petra onto his lap, brushed the hair from her face, and kissed her brow. She opened her eyes at his touch, jerked her hand up his chest and splayed her fingers on his cheek.

"Piitalaat," Maratse whispered. "I'm going to take you home."

"Yes," she said.

Gaba nodded for Danielsen and Atii to step to one side.

"We're going to need photos," he said. "Once we get them to the helicopter, I need you both to stay here. Document everything."

"You're taking them back on the same chopper with him?" Atii whispered. "With Jaqqa?"

"No," Gaba said. "I think we can stretch Simonsen's budget just a little more. Besides," he said with a firm twist of his jaw. "I can talk to Jaqqa while they fly back."

"Do you have him?" Maratse said. Gaba hesitated as Maratse looked at him. "Gaba?"

"Yes," he said. "We have him."

Maratse looked at Atii. "Will you stay with her?"

"Of course," she said, as Maratse helped Petra into Atii's arms.

"David?" Petra said. "You can't leave me."

"It's okay, Piitalaat. I won't be long."

"What are you going to do?"

"Don't think about it, Petra," he said. Maratse raised his arm and Gaba pulled him to his feet.

He looked at Petra as he found his balance and then stumbled across the rocky floor to pick up his rifle.

"Maratse," Gaba said. "This isn't a good idea."

Gaba swore and followed Maratse as he slung the rifle over his shoulder and took slow steps towards the cable car.

"We have him in custody," Gaba said. "He'll be tried, and convicted. We have plenty of evidence. Hey, listen to me." Gaba gripped Maratse by the shoulder as they reached the cable car dock. "He'll get life. That's fifteen years, minimum."

"He doesn't deserve life," Maratse said.

"Stop."

"You're going to stop me?" Maratse looked Gaba in the eye.

"I can't let you do it. You're a police officer."

"I'm retired." Maratse brushed free of Gaba's grip and stepped inside the cable car.

Chapter 25

Maratse gripped the handrail as the cable car reduced speed to a slow swing above the dock at the camp. He nodded as Gaba took his arm and guided him over the gap between the car and the wooden dock. Maratse took small steps towards a figure kneeling on the ground.

"Peter," Gaba said, as he walked around Maratse. "Take the car back up, and help them bring Petra down."

"Sure," he said with a glance at Maratse.

Maratse ignored him, concentrating on one measured step after another until he stood in front of Jaqqa.

"You're alive," Jaqqa said, as he lifted his head.

"And you're free to go," Maratse said.

"No." Jaqqa twisted on the ground. He frowned at Gaba as the SRU Sergeant pulled out his knife and cut the plastic ties binding his wrists.

"They're not pressing charges," he said.

"But I'm in your custody."

"Not anymore, you're free to go." Gaba closed the knife and waved as Peter watched from the cable car.

The clank and loud tick of the cable turning in the drums made it difficult to talk. Maratse stared at Jaqqa until the drums slowed and the sound stopped. The cable car had reached the entrance to the mine. It would be returning soon. Petra would be with them. Maratse nodded at Gaba.

"Now," he said.

"Now *what?*" Jaqqa rose to his feet.

"It's time for you to go."

"Go where? On the helicopter?"

Gaba shook his head. "That's for Sergeant Jensen. You'll have to make other arrangements."

He leaned to one side and stared out onto the frozen fjord. Almost black against the ice, the snow scooter cast a shadow in the moonlight. It was just visible. Jaqqa looked in the same direction. When Maratse slipped his fingers around the sling of his rifle, he started to run. Gaba waited until he was past the first building before he spoke.

"Did you kill Aksel?"

"*Eeqqi.*"

"I didn't think so. There was a video camera. We haven't seen much, but Salik was in it."

Maratse worked the bolt of the rifle to check the bullet in the chamber. When he looked up Jaqqa was scrambling down the rocks. He watched him leap onto the ice. Maratse took a slow, painful step forwards.

"You'll never catch him," Gaba said.

"Maybe not."

"And you know it's life if you do. Who will look after Petra?"

"So long as he lives," Maratse said, "she'll never recover."

"So, you're doing this for her?"

"*Iiji.*"

Gaba sighed. "I'll have to arrest you."

"Call Simonsen," Maratse said. He almost smiled. "He'd like that."

"We'll see," Gaba said. He flicked his finger towards the ice. "How good a shot are you? He's almost at the snow scooter."

Maratse shrugged and took another painful step

forwards. Jaqqa slowed as he reached the snow scooter. Maratse leaned against the last building in the camp before the rocks and the ice. He caught his breath as Jaqqa slid his leg over the seat and sat down.

"Christ, Maratse," Gaba said, as he ran to the building. "Show me the keys or shoot him. I can't let him get away."

"Just watch," Maratse said, as he lowered the rifle.

There was no cry, or scream, Jaqqa said nothing as his body flipped backwards off the snow scooter as a short burst of lightning blazed into his body.

"Wait here," Maratse said, as he stumbled down the rocks and onto the ice. He walked around the softer ice, winding a longer route to the snow scooter than the one he had taken on the way in. He heard the cable car start its descent as he closed the distance between him and Jaqqa.

"What did you do?" Jaqqa said, as Maratse leaned against the back of the snow scooter.

"I once knew a Chinese man," Maratse said. "He liked electricity and did some things to me that I'd like to forget. But I see the scars in the mirror, feel them in my legs, and remember them in my dreams." Maratse grimaced as he shifted his weight from one leg to the other.

"Why are you telling me this?" Jaqqa said.

"Because the hardest thing for me is not the scars, not even the pain, it's wondering if he will ever do it again. As long as he is alive, there is that chance. I can't let that happen to Piitalaat. Do you understand?"

"You're not going to let me go, are you?"

"*Eeqqi*," Maratse said and shook his head.

Maratse and Jaqqa turned at the sound of shouting in the camp. Someone had found the switch to turn on the halogen lights. The buildings reflected the light onto the snow between them, and the light from the lamps closest to the ice caught the reflective stripes of Petra's ski suit as she slipped down the rocks and splashed through the water at the edge of the ice. Maratse started towards her, stopping as he saw Gaba leap onto the ice and pull Petra into his arms. She kicked at him, her heels thumping softly on his shins as she jabbed at his vest with her elbows.

"David," she screamed. "Don't, David."

Jaqqa kicked at Maratse's wounded leg, throwing him off balance. Maratse grunted as he sprawled on the ice. The rifle skittered out of his grasp. Jaqqa lunged for it, kicking at Maratse's hands.

"David," Petra screamed. She threw back her head and caught Gaba in the nose. He dropped her and she scrabbled to her feet, slipping across the ice in wet socks until she found her footing, and her strength. Petra ran towards them.

"You should have left me in custody," Jaqqa said, as he stood up. He pointed the barrel of the rifle at Maratse's chest. "You could have killed me with that battery trick." Jaqqa laughed, and then turned his back on Maratse and aimed at Petra, shifting his aim slightly as Petra slipped on the ice.

"No," Maratse said, as he pushed himself onto his feet. "This isn't how it ends."

"Quiet, old man," Jaqqa said.

Maratse heard three things – the slap of Petra's feet across the ice, the first click of the trigger tightening in Jaqqa's grasp, and his grandfather's voice on the wind.

Now, Qilingatsaq.

Maratse gripped the knife from the scabbard lashed to the scooter and thrust it into Jaqqa's side. Jaqqa dropped the rifle and Maratse pulled the knife out. He stabbed him again and again until Jaqqa stopped squirming and his blood pooled on the ice. Petra froze at the sight, dropped to her knees, and pressed her hands to her face.

"It's okay, Piitalaat," Maratse said. "He can't hurt you anymore."

Maratse closed his eyes. He could feel the vibration of feet pounding along the ice. He felt hands on his body, and he tried to open his eyes, but he was weak. He heard Gaba's voice, and then another, the new man, Peter, perhaps. Something about *loss of blood* and *very weak*. He could have told them that.

He felt something else, thin fingers tugging at his own as Gaba and Peter lifted him and carried him across the ice to the mining camp. *Piitalaat.* They were her fingers. There for a moment and then gone, and then he was lying down on a seat. There was a scratch of metal. He tried to open his eyes, but it was white, just white, and then the whining and the roaring began. He lifted his hand, heard the man's voice again. *Was it Peter?* And then he searched for her, found her fingers and gripped them. He would never let go. Never again. She was back. They would be together, always.

Maratse woke inside a white room, a tiny ward off the main corridor of Uummannaq hospital. He could smell tobacco. Old smoke. He searched the room and saw Simonsen leaning in the corner. The Chief of

Uummannaq police was smiling, and Maratse felt a twinge in his stomach that had nothing to do with being shot in the thigh. He started to speak but Simonsen shushed him.

"Just a second," he said, and turned up the volume on the radio.

He watched Maratse as they listened to the news broadcast in Greenlandic first, followed by a Danish version. Maratse understood both. He was one step ahead of the Chief, but he realised it was likely to be the last time.

Maratse couldn't remember ever hearing Malik Uutaaq speak Danish in public, but his accent and pronunciation were perfect, although he declined to comment when asked about his personal thoughts on diversity in Greenland.

"You've heard the official statement," he said, his voice booming through the radio, his tone strong and commanding, defying the radio host to press him any further.

"Can you believe it?" Simonsen said. "Uutaaq's has been given a ministerial position in Nivi Winther's government. It's a mistake." Simonsen laughed. "She must be mad. "

"Or clever," Maratse said.

"Well, you would know all about that, eh?" Simonsen sat at the end of Maratse's bed.

"Where is Piitalaat?"

"She's next door. She's waiting to see you." Simonsen paused. "*Piitalaat*. That's how you knew. Isn't it?"

"*Iiji.*"

"And you couldn't just tell me?"

Maratse thought for a moment, and then he

remembered the watch on his wrist, the second hand thudding for every wasted moment. "There wasn't time," he said.

"Well, you're going to have plenty of that for a while," Simonsen said. "You killed someone, Maratse." he lifted his hand. "Extenuating circumstances, I will agree, but you obstructed justice and took the law into your own hands. Do you remember Natsi Hermansen? He says you tortured him. He's pressing charges. As are the two men you beat up in Saattut."

Maratse closed his eyes. He had forgotten about them.

"I did what I had to do," he said.

"You did. Like you always do."

The wheels beneath the bed squealed as Simonsen stood up.

"I have two funerals to go to. Anton is burying two thirds of his family." He sighed. "It makes no sense."

Maratse nodded. He waited until Simonsen was at the door.

"How long?" he asked.

"What do you mean?"

"Before you arrest me?"

Maratse had the impression that Simonsen would have spat, if they had been outside. "You still have friends in high places. The Commissioner has pulled some strings, again. You'll be under house arrest until the case is ready for court." Simonsen shook his head. "I'll be watching, Maratse. Closer now than before. You don't leave that house. Do you understand?"

"*Iiji.*"

Maratse waited until he was gone, and then threw

back the sheets. He held his breath as he swung his legs over the side. The floor was cold beneath his feet. He saw a pair of slippers beside the bed and squirmed his feet into them. The grip wasn't quite as firm as the soles of Buuti's *kamikker*, but they would do. Maratse shuffled to the door.

There was a small crowd in the corridor, faces he knew. Maratse felt a tiny hand clasp his and looked down at Nanna; her blonde hair tickled his skin as she tugged his hand to her face.

"Gently, Nanna," Sisse said. She pressed her hand against Maratse's cheek and collected Nanna into her arms. "We'll see you later," she said.

Buuti was next. She wrapped her arms around Maratse's body, hugging and squeezing with a sense of urgency that could have been therapeutic or disciplinary. The look on Karl's face suggested it was best not to ask.

"Buuti," Karl said, as he placed his hand on her shoulder. "We can see him later. There are others..."

Buuti wiped her eyes on Maratse's hospital gown and pressed her hand against his chest.

"Come home soon," she said. "Both of you."

"*Iiji.*"

Karl pointed at the door to the next room and Maratse shuffled towards it. He almost turned around at the sight of a pink-haired young woman. She had studs beneath her bottom lip. In the soft light of the room, Maratse thought they might have been tusks.

"This is Tertu," Qitu said, as he crossed the room to shake Maratse's hand. "We're here for Salik's funeral. She and Petra have been talking. When you're ready, we'd like to talk to you too."

"Are you writing an article?"

"Yes. Tertu wants to tell her story," he said, as Tertu nodded. "She feels she can tell it now, thanks to you."

"Hm," Maratse said.

The woman hugged Petra, and then took Qitu's hand, pulling him out of the room. The door closed softly behind them, and they were alone.

Petra fiddled with the drip taped to the back of her hand, brushed her hair behind her ears and smiled.

"It's okay, David," she said. "I'm alright."

He sat down on the bed and took her hand. The weave of the dressings was rough to the touch and there were spots of blood seeping through the white bandages. Her hand trembled.

"You're sure?"

"Yes," she said. "With your help, I'll be okay. But it might take some time."

Author's Note

Greenland is the largest island in the world, but with roughly 56,000 inhabitants, its population is smaller than the city of Galveston, Texas. The capital of Nuuk has a population of roughly 15,000 people. Some settlements have fewer than one hundred residents. There are no roads connecting the towns, villages, and settlements. Transport to and from the inhabited areas is predominantly serviced by planes with short take off and landing capabilities, helicopters, and boats. In the areas where the sea ice is thick enough, Greenlanders can travel across the ice in cars, and by snow scooters and dog sledges.

Constable David Maratse's fictive Greenland is affected by the same limitations of the real Greenland. His fictive stories are inspired by some events and many places that exist in Greenland. Most place names are the same, such as Nuuk, and Uummannaq, but used fictitiously. The settlement of Inussuk does not exist, although observant readers looking at a map will be able to take a good guess at where it might be found.

Chris
November 2018
Denmark

Acknowledgements

I would like to thank Isabel Dennis-Muir for her invaluable editing skills and feedback on the manuscript. While several people have contributed to *We Shall Be Monsters*, the mistakes and inaccuracies are all my own.

Chris
November 2018
Denmark

About the Author

Christoffer Petersen is the author's pen name. He lives in Denmark. Chris started writing stories about Greenland while teaching in Qaanaaq, the largest village in the very north of Greenland – the population peaked at 600 during the two years he lived there. Chris spent a total of seven years in Greenland, teaching in remote communities and at the Police Academy in the capital of Nuuk.

Chris continues to be inspired by the vast icy wilderness of the Arctic and his books have a common setting in the region, with a Scandinavian influence. He has also watched enough Bourne movies to no longer be surprised by the plot, but not enough to get bored.

You can find Chris in Denmark or online here:

www.christoffer-petersen.com

By the same author:

THE GREENLAND CRIME SERIES
featuring Constable David Maratse

Seven Graves, One Winter *book 1*
Blood Floe *book 2*
Feral *book 3*

SHORT STORIES from the same series
featuring Constable David Maratse

Katabatic *story 1*
Container *story 2*
Tupilaq *story 3*
The Last Flight *story 4*
The Heart that was a Wild Garden *story 5*

THE GREENLAND TRILOGY
featuring Konstabel Fenna Brongaard

The Ice Star *book 1*
In the Shadow of the Mountain *book 2*
The Shaman's House *book 3*

THE DARK ADVENT SERIES
featuring Police Commissioner Petra "Piitalaat" Jensen
set in Greenland

The Calendar Man *book 1*
The Twelfth Night *book 2*

Made in United States
North Haven, CT
06 February 2022

15744365R00131